What Happened to
SOPHIE
WILDER

a novel

by CHRISTOPHER R. BEHA

Tin House Books
Portland, Oregon & New York, New York

Published by Tin House Books, Portland, Oregon, and New York, New York

Distributed to the trade by Publishers Group West, 1700 Fourth St., Berkeley, CA 94710, www.pgw.com

Library of Congress Cataloging-in-Publication Data

Beha, Christopher R.
 What happened to Sophie Wilder : a novel / by Christopher R. Beha.
— 1st U.S. ed.
    p. cm.
 ISBN 978-1-935639-31-2 (trade paper) — ISBN 978-1-935639-32-9 (ebook)
 I. Title.
 PS3602.E375W47 2012
 813'.6—dc23

                                            2012005758

First U.S. edition 2012
Printed in the USA
Interior design by Diane Chonette
www.tinhouse.com

What Happened to Sophie Wilder contains phrases from Wallace Stevens's "Country Words," T. S. Eliot's "Ash Wednesday," Immanuel Kant's *Critique of Pure Reason*, Robert Frost's "Stars," and Rainer Maria Rilke's "Autumn Day."

To my parents

"When you write my epitaph, you must say I was the loneliest person who ever lived."

—ELIZABETH BISHOP, in a letter to Robert Lowell

"If you don't believe in God, how do you believe in a fucking book?"

—ROBERTO BOLAÑO, 2666

PART ONE

The Stars Above

1

BEFORE I CAME to stay at the Manse I lived in an old townhouse on the north side of Washington Square, where my cousin Max and I rented rooms from a middle-aged German man named Gerhard Gottlieb, the uncle of one of Max's old flames. I was never entirely sure what business Gerhard was in, but he was usually out of the country, and he gave us the run of the place in his absence, provided we walked his dog, a purebred boxer named Ginger, and fed the tropical fish in his enormous Victorian aquarium. Max and I were the only ones paying rent, but there were often two or three others staying on the vacant floor above us. We were all "in the arts," as we liked to say with intense but undirected irony, which is what left us free to take Ginger out during the day and to spend our nights entertaining ourselves in that old house, drinking bourbon and smoking those thin, elegant joints that we all rolled so easily.

Max was the film critic for a local weekly. He didn't like movies much, at least not the ones he was called upon to review, but he felt strongly that a critic who wasn't part of the conversation—at a certain point in the night we could use such terms in earnest—was no critic at all. The artist was free to work in isolation, even to cultivate it. But the critic was an explainer. His job depended on an audience, and the audience went to the movies. So Max said on those evenings when an unseen judge called us to defend the manner in which we spent our days.

The part about cultivating isolation he aimed at me. And it was true that no one had read my novel when it came out a few months before. But this wasn't by virtue of any aesthetic stratagem. I would have been more than happy with an audience. My publisher had paid me well and put its energy, as they call it, behind the book. I'd been reviewed where one hopes to be reviewed; some of the notices had even been good. Max and I share the same last name—our fathers are brothers, or were while mine was still alive—and there had been brief talk, much of it generated by Max himself, about the Blakemans representing some new cultural moment. That had all passed after my book sank quietly from view. Outside the world of mean-spirited media blogs no one had any idea who we were. Max secretly faulted me for this, though in truth people were simply tired of comfortable young white guys from New York. I couldn't blame them; I was tired of us, too.

For all that disappointment, the money had been real, and Gerhard barely charged rent, so I didn't need much to get by. I could live on my advance while I figured out what came next. I understood that I shouldn't expect too much from whatever that turned out to be. I'd been given my big chance—more than most get—and now I was on my own.

In the meantime, we spent long hours in that house, talking about the Grand Gesture, whether it nowadays existed, of what it might consist if it did. We wanted badly to believe it was still possible to live off ideas, except when we wanted badly to believe that it was no longer possible, since then the failure to do so was not our own, not caused by a lack of discipline or talent or by the fact that we didn't finally want the things we wanted as much as we thought we wanted them.

In truth we were quickly reaching—had likely enough already reached—the age where it no longer made sense to talk about "promise." It was around this time that I remarked to Max that no matter what we now achieved no one would say, "He's so young." Precocity had passed us by.

"After twenty-eight," I said sadly, "you're judged on your merits."

"Unless one of us dies," Max corrected me. "Then they'll all say, 'He was so young.'"

All of this is by way of an honest accounting of where things stood for me on the early autumn evening when I came home from dinner to a crowded party and found Sophie Wilder sitting on the half-collapsed leather couch near that antique aquarium in the far corner of Gerhard's living room.

I had been thinking a lot about Sophie—she's long been someone I think about—so I had an immediate sense, one I never entirely shook throughout all that followed, that I had summoned her to me. So far as I knew, she'd been gone from New York since her split with Tom, and now she was here. When I'd heard that her marriage was over, I wanted to reach out, but I wasn't sure how to go about it. Then I'd learned that she'd left town. There had been some speculation over her whereabouts. She was at a writers' colony—not Yaddo or MacDowell, but one of those obscure ones out West. She had gone to work for an NGO in Africa. She was living in a convent near her childhood home in Connecticut.

For all that, it made sense to me that she should appear now on Gerhard's couch. I felt no surprise as I crossed the open space that occupied most of the house's first floor, only a shiver of delight and an appreciation for the narrative shapeliness of it. That which was supposed to happen had happened.

"Charlie," she called, and she floated up to meet me. She had grown her black hair out long, and it softened a bit the usually sharp lines of her pale face. Otherwise she seemed unchanged from the girl I'd known. She leaned in to kiss me on the cheek.

"How are you?" I asked.

She took a step back, leaving her left hand to rest carelessly against my collarbone as if she'd forgotten it there, and she considered the question. This was something I only then remembered about her—the habit she had of taking everything I said seriously, even small talk, so that I wanted always to be my best self around her. I remembered too how this habit occasionally became suffocating, as the constant demand to be your best self naturally does.

"Isn't it a funny thing?" she said, as if she'd been caught out at something. "I came into the city for the day, just to go to some galleries, and I ran into your cousin on the street."

Max came in from the kitchen then, carrying two drinks, an unlit cigarette in the crook of his lower lip. Sophie withdrew her hand from my shoulder, bringing it to her face almost protectively, and I thought: *Yes, Max.* Another thing about her that I'd almost forgotten.

• • •

In the beginning, there was only the name. Ten of us had been admitted to the Introduction to Fiction workshop my freshman fall at New Hampton, a small liberal arts college in central New Jersey, but only nine arrived for the first class. Our professor, a near-famous novelist, called our names alphabetically, finishing with Sophie Wilder. No one answered. The following week she was still not there, and we started to wonder.

An otherwise undistinguished school, New Hampton was known for the novelists and poets it had gathered to teach its undergraduates, and many aspirants turned down more prestigious colleges to study with them. After enrolling, you had to submit a second application for the writing program, so that a student who had come to New Hampton solely for these workshops could still be shut out of them. To those of us who'd made the cut, it was hard to imagine someone had been accepted and not shown up.

The third week, she appeared.

Even if she hadn't missed our first two classes, she would have stood out to me. I want to say that she looked more adult than the rest of us, more experienced, but this isn't quite so. In fact, she seemed terribly uncomfortable, as though there against her will. One might have expected such a person to be shy or unprepared, but when our professor asked her a question she answered with articulate care. She had considered opinions about all the work we discussed that week, but she would have let those opinions go unspoken had she not been forced to participate. She became more comfortable as the semester passed, but this pattern continued unchanged: she never commented voluntarily, but she always had something to say.

The rest of us spoke as much as we could, mostly to impress our professor, which turned out to be little use.

Sophie was the only one he took seriously. Whatever the cause of her early absences, he didn't hold them against her. As the weeks passed, he pushed more and more frequently for her thoughts, often giving her the last word on our work. It was difficult not to resent her for this, though she did nothing to ask for this treatment and took no apparent pleasure in it.

In the second month of the semester, Sophie's turn to submit work came, and she distributed a seventy-five-page story to the class. Here was another thing to resent. Not that she was capable of writing at such length—though there was that; few of us could sustain a narrative much longer than ten pages—but that she would impose such writing on us. Her thoughtful responses throughout the semester now seemed designed to justify this imposition. And justify they did: after all her attention, it would have been shameful to show up to class without a proper reaction to this stack of paper, a novella really, too thick for a staple or a standard paper clip.

I sat out in the courtyard near my dorm the day before that week's workshop, smoking Parliaments and reading those pages. It was a kind of gothic tale about a young boy and girl—brother and sister, though this was never said outright—living by their wits in a large, empty mansion in the woods. Their parents were never mentioned, their absence never explained. In the middle of the story, a pack of wild animals surrounds the house, keeping the children from foraging for food in the woods. The animals howl through the night, so that the girl and boy can't sleep. Days pass, the cupboards empty, and the two children sag with exhaustion. Finally, the boy descends without explanation to the cellar, where a shotgun with ammunition is waiting for him. This gun, the story suggests, is some kind of legacy the boy has avoided taking up before then. But now he has no choice. The boy brings the gun outside and, over the course of ten pages, he shoots and kills all the animals. Then he goes upstairs to his bed. While he sleeps, the girl digs a pit in which she buries the dead. When she has finished, she washes herself deliberately, with an air of ceremony, before heading to the bedroom she shares with the boy. She stands over him, watching him sleep. He has left the shotgun—*his* shotgun, now—leaning against the door frame. She takes it up and shoots the boy. Then she curls up beside him and closes her eyes.

In class the next day I looked at the author of this strange tale and discovered that she was beautiful. This fact had been slow to reveal itself because, for all her beauty, Sophie wasn't quite pretty. To find her so attractive suggested a kind of refinement on my part, I thought, like appreciating some quietly elegant story that bored the rest of the class. No one could possibly have called her "cute," which was how desirable girls were universally described on campus. But she made the cute girls seem meretricious in their cuteness, with her boyishly short dark hair, her skin pale except where it was lightly freckled, on those high cheeks that despite their fullness seemed to struggle under the weight of her eyes. Her nose was long and sharp, and I suspect that this feature concealed her beauty from me at first, though it was a key to its richness once discovered. The light in the October air was still summer-sharp but turning somber, and she wore a thick, blue cable-knit sweater, out of style and overlarge, something a father throws over a little girl when they've both been surprised by the cold. The sleeves were pushed up above her elbows and both forearms were lined with wide wooden bracelets of every shade of green and gray.

Throughout the half hour we spent on her work she kept her eyes on the table in front of her. It was almost immediately clear that we were all impressed, but she seemed desperate for the discussion to be over. I tried to respond as she would have, with carefully considered remarks, but I lost the thread of my thoughts while watching her squirm on the other side of the room. When I came to myself I found that I had been babbling on, and the rest of the class looked nearly as embarrassed as she did. I trailed off then, and our professor said a few closing words before letting us go.

She caught up to me as I crossed the few blocks that separated the Fine Arts Center from the rest of campus, and she shadowed me silently as my shame deepened. She no longer seemed nervous or uncomfortable, only a little annoyed, though she was the one intruding on me.

"I'm Sophie," she said eventually, without prompting, as if it had just then occurred to her that we might talk while we walked.

"Charlie," I answered.

"You're from the city."

This was not a question but a statement, one not entirely directed at me, as though she were filling in my backstory while I listened. We had given our hometowns when introducing ourselves on the first day of class, but she hadn't been there, so I didn't know when she'd learned this about me.

"Did you like growing up in New York?"

"I'm glad I'm here now," I said.

My father had been sick throughout my high school years, and he'd died only a few months before I headed off to college. I felt guilty about leaving my mother alone, though I couldn't imagine staying with her. She'd been unhappy long before she'd had any reason for it that I could understand, and after my father's death her mute suffering filled the atmosphere of that apartment, of her life.

"You like the Beats?"

This too had come from class, when we had been asked to name our "influences." Max had given me his copy of *Dharma Bums* a few years earlier, around the time that my father got sick, and I had thrown myself into Kerouac and Ginsberg and Burroughs and even Gary Snyder and Lucien Carr and Gregory Corso; they had been a great solace, for they suggested the life I might have some day, when being orphaned would be a kind of existential condition from which to make great work, rather than just another species of loss.

"Burroughs is pretty good," she went on, making a concession I hadn't demanded. "Most of the rest is shit."

She expected a response, but I had none, so she continued.

"There's no control, no sense of form. They romanticize their methods, as if we should read *how* they wrote instead of *what* they wrote. Eventually it all turns sentimental, like a conversation with a sloppy drunk."

No one I knew—certainly no one our age—spoke this way about books. She made this kind of talk seem like one of the great excitements of our new near-adulthood lives, like being able to spend our days and nights as we wished.

She smiled, waiting for me to fight back on behalf of these writers I was supposed to admire. But the authority of her tone overwhelmed me. To be honest, I didn't read all that much then, although books had been prized in my home and I'd said from a young age that I wanted to write. Mostly I read what Max told me to read, since he was a year older and his tastes were beyond reproach.

"I see what you mean," I said, which was a weak start but true. As soon as she'd pronounced her verdict on the books I'd lived with for the past three or four years I understood it to be just. But my concession disappointed her. She expected a defense. It took a long time to understand this about Sophie: she never wanted submission; she wanted an evenhanded fight. It didn't much matter to her whether she won or lost.

"Who do you like?" I asked.

"Nabokov."

"*Lolita*?"

I had started the book a year earlier, again on Max's recommendation, and I had expected something in line with the other novels he'd been giving me. I had set it down when its elegance failed to turn lurid, and I hadn't yet picked it back up.

"Sure," she said. "But I like *Pale Fire* better. And *Ada*. Some of the early Russian ones, too, like *The Defense*. I spent most of last year reading Proust, who put just as much of his life in his books as Kerouac did. But he believed in craft."

This would have been difficult to take from someone else, but it was somehow clear that she wasn't showing off.

"Sounds like you prefer the legend of the cork-lined room to the legend of the typewriter roll and the Benzedrine."

She laughed only briefly, but it was an honest laugh.

We didn't say all that much for the rest of our walk. I asked where she was heading, and I discovered that we lived in the same building, though I hadn't seen her there before. I felt then for the first time that unsurprised feeling that returned when I found her on Gerhard's couch, as if from then on whoever was writing us down would take care to keep us near each other, to return us to each other's stories, even when all the forces of convention and plausibility spoke against it. She took a pack of cigarettes from her bag and offered me one. While we smoked and walked, we occasionally passed people we knew. One of us would stop to talk and the other would wait, and in this way we went from being two people who had happened to leave class at the same time to two people going somewhere together. If I could be just one thing now, that would be it: someone going somewhere with Sophie Wilder.

• • •

There wasn't a particular occasion for the party at Gerhard's that night—we were often celebrating in those days, and there was rarely an occasion—but a pretty good crowd had assembled. Sophie and Max and I stood for a moment within it, facing one other beside Gerhard's aquarium. Max gave Sophie the drinks, freeing his hands to light his cigarette. Then he took one back and touched his glass to hers.

So far as I knew, Sophie hadn't had a drink in years, since taking to marriage and God. But perhaps all that was over, now that she and Tom had separated. As for Max, he always stayed Max—if anything, became more Max-like— so that it was natural that he should depend on everyone to be just as he'd always known them to be.

Sophie took a long sip from her glass and leaned lightly against him. I noticed then that they were both drunk. I took a cigarette from Max before heading to the kitchen.

There were four or five people assembled there, none I'd ever seen before, all surrounding a tall, thin guy about my age wearing a bow tie and a tuxedo shirt with plastic studs over an outlandishly tight pair of black jeans. His mustache—"my mustaches," I could almost hear him calling it—was waxed.

"So I asked Wes what kind of palette he was thinking of using this time," he was saying as I entered. "I told him I really dig the *palettes* that he chooses."

I pushed through the crowd to the cabinets and the sink.

"Dude," the guy in the tuxedo shirt said to me. "I think we're supposed to use those."

He gestured with a tattooed finger to a sleeve of red plastic cups on the counter.

"Thanks," I said, continuing my search in the cabinet for a clean glass. "I live here."

I mixed a vodka-soda, more vodka than soda, which I drank while standing over the sink. I was suddenly very tired of these parties that occupied so much of my life. Or else I realized suddenly that I had grown tired of them long ago. I wasn't sure if I was done with them because Sophie had appeared or if Sophie had appeared because I was done with them and so ready for her to come back.

In the living room, Max was introducing Sophie to Jeff, a fact-checker at his magazine.

"So," Jeff said, "you knew Blakeman before he was famous. What on earth was he like?"

Everyone called Max "Blakeman." Sometimes even I did it, though it was my own name.

"I was always famous," Max insisted, "even when no one had heard of me."

This line had been funny once, before it looked possible that we might truly become famous. It seemed that it was funny again now that this possibility had passed.

Max's college roommate Rick Tanner, who now worked in a gallery in Chelsea, lightly set Jeff aside.

"Sophie Wilder," he said, and he kissed her on both cheeks. "Fucking hell, it's been years. I heard you got married."

"We split up," Sophie said.

"You know who else split up?" Rick asked, speaking no longer to Sophie but to the others collecting around her. "Henry and Klara."

"They seemed like a perfect couple," some dutiful straight man protested.

"She practically had her head in the oven," Rick said. "I mean, Henry's the Ted Hughes of management consultants."

Everyone but Sophie laughed at this, and I took the opportunity to approach her.

"How have you been?"

"You already asked me that," she said.

"And you still haven't answered."

"Fair enough. Let's table the matter pending further review. How about yourself?"

I'd been doing well enough, all things considered. But I didn't tell her that. Instead I said, "I've missed you."

It was a ridiculous thing to tell her after all these years. But true. And I missed her more now that she was right there in front of me. She raised a hand and placed her palm against my cheek. Then she brought it down and said, "It's a nice house," and the spell was broken.

"Gerhard, the guy who owns it, says Henry James lived here. But there's no plaque or anything. Probably it's bullshit."

"James hated Washington Square when he came back to the States," Sophie said. "It made him feel like he'd been amputated."

I'd never heard this before, but it was just the kind of thing that Sophie knew. I was preparing my response when the room fell quiet. We both turned to see Eddie Hartley, an old friend Max and I had known since our days at St. Albert's, now a struggling actor who appeared in commercials and an occasional *Law and Order* episode, standing on the leather ottoman. He began to read Wallace Stevens from a book he'd taken off one of the shelves:

> *I sang a canto in a canton,*
> *Cunning-coo, O, cuckoo cock . . .*

The crowd around Eddie urged him on. He finished and bowed facetiously. Then he looked over to me.

"Your turn, Charlie."

These performances—impromptu readings of modern poetry that were at the same time ironic mockeries of the sort of party where such impromptu readings might genuinely occur—were a common feature of our nights. I hadn't thought much about them before, but I was embarrassed for Sophie to see a joke made of things that had mattered so much to us. Eddie handed me the book. I stood on the ottoman and gave a humorless reading of "The Emperor of Ice Cream" that took the life out of the crowd, much as I had hoped it would. I stepped down with the book still in my hand and headed back to where I had been standing with Sophie. But she had disappeared.

In the kitchen I found only the same group of strangers, collected in a conspiratorial huddle around the oven. As I entered, a few stepped aside to reveal the one in the bow tie. He held a screwdriver, with which he had removed two knobs from the stove. Now he was working on a third. When he saw me watching he stopped.

"Sorry, man," he said. "Just fucking around."

"Be my guest," I told him. "We don't cook."

I poured another vodka.

Back in the living room, I asked Jeff if he knew where Sophie had gone.

"I think she left with Max," he said.

"You're up," I told him, handing him the book of poems.

Then I took a seat on the couch beside the aquarium to watch Gerhard's beautiful fish and ask myself, not for the first time or the last, What happened to Sophie Wilder?

2

THE PHONE WAS already ringing when she came home from mass that morning, and she let it go a while as she settled in. She crossed through the living room—the "common room," Tom still sometimes called it, as if he and Sophie lived in a dorm, or as if the entire place weren't common to them—and arrived at her desk after three or four rings. They had the landline only for the Internet connection, and they never used this phone, which was the cheapest thing they could find, off-white with a cord and a cradle and an oversized touchpad, as if one of them were going blind. In another setting it might have seemed knowing or campy, but here it looked bluntly functional, like most of the apartment; Sophie lacked the domestic instinct, and Tom was too rarely home to bother over such things.

Nevertheless, the number was listed, and they occasionally got calls, mostly solicitations. The phone sat on her desk, near at hand, and if it rang while she was working she might pick it up and drop it back down without a word. She was often tempted to unplug it, but Tom would complain if he came home and found it that way.

What if there's an emergency?

Who's going to call? she would ask. No one has the number.

I do, Tom would say.

You can call my cell.

But it's never on.

Which was fair enough. She turned off her phone each morning before mass and often forgot about it for the rest of the day. She wrote grant proposals for small charities, and her clients—ostensibly nonprofit directors but mostly just individuals with causes, sometimes nuns or parish priests seeking to serve their congregations in ways the archdiocese hadn't provided for in the budget—had little need to be in touch while she made their cases to various corporate foundations. There was occasional fieldwork involved, trips to shelters and soup kitchens, once to the home of an old man, a former violent felon, who collected clothes for parolees to wear to job interviews. But mostly she sat at her desk all day as she had before, and she didn't want to make herself entirely available to the world. A certain kind of disconnection felt necessary, though she couldn't explain to Tom why this was so.

She worked in the same marbled notebooks she'd always used, and she opened one now while the phone rang for the tenth or eleventh time. They had no answering machine, so it might continue indefinitely. Perhaps it really was something important. More likely one of those recordings. She wondered if the computer cut off at some point, or if it went on forever.

Once she'd decided to answer, she moved with slow deliberation, daring the caller to give up on her. She closed the notebook, which she'd bought along with half a dozen others three weeks before, after running through her last batch. She waited for the phone to sound out once more and then picked it up midring.

"Hello?"

A pause on the other end, as if for the drawing of breath. Later, when she told the story, trying to make something out of it, she said that she knew in that moment who was there. But who can say what intimations she really felt?

"Thomas?"

Her husband's name came through to her, weak and uncertain. Then she did know, though she'd never heard this voice before. And she knew that she'd been waiting for the call.

"Tom is at the office," she said. When no response came, she added, "You can call back later if you'd like. He usually gets in around midnight."

This was not an exaggeration, but an outer estimate. Tom hadn't come home before nine in weeks, and he was often still at the office when Sophie went to sleep.

"Can you give me his number at work?"

She didn't mean to leave the man in suspense, but she took a moment deciding what to do, what Tom would want her to do. He filled the silence apologetically.

"This is his father."

Something about the voice wasn't right. He's drunk, she thought. I can't let him call Tom in this condition. As if in answer to her suspicion, he continued slowly, sounding out his words, letting each stand a moment on its own.

"It's an emergency."

Sophie gave him the number, but only because Tom would want to handle it himself, would want her to have as little as possible to do with the man, and because this seemed the quickest way to get him off the phone. After he'd hung up, she sat at her desk, receiver in hand, until the phone started to make that obnoxious sound it made when left off the hook, a plea for attention from the world of objects. She had waited years for a chance to speak to him, and now the chance had passed. Tom would do his best to make sure there wasn't another.

The notebook sat dead on her desk, and she left it there. She opened the sliding door and stepped out into the sticky heat of their small concrete terrace. From twenty-eight stories up she looked at New York, to which the late-morning humidity seemed applied like a wrapping of gauze. The sky above was cloudless, empty but curiously pale.

Over the years, she had given many hours of thought to Tom's father, wondering how it would feel if she still had a parent alive in the world, always present, and she never spoke to him. She and Tom had a long understanding that she would not ask about him, and she'd abided by it. Tom gave no sign that the man's continued existence interested him at all, but Sophie couldn't really believe this was true. For her own part, her father-in-law was among the most persistent puzzles in her life. She marveled now at the fact that she'd spoken with him only a moment before, even more at the idea that she had hurried him off the phone when she'd finally had a chance to speak with him. She regretted this rush in the uneasy way that she occasionally regretted doing something that she nonetheless felt had been right. Still, she wasn't sure what she would have asked him, had she felt free to ask anything.

Sophie worked a cigarette from the soft pack in her front pocket and lit it with a match. Since she'd started again, she used only matches, because each pack was always her last, a fifty-cent lighter always an unsound investment. A year into this relapse, she could still become light-headed and pleasantly queasy after smoking just one. When she eventually finished it, flicked it over the rail, and leaned to watch it disappear, she felt a gratifying vertigo. The butt twisted elegantly, leaving a light trail of ash in its wake. Then it seemed to catch on a bit of air and slow in its fall, and she imagined herself in its place. She swung her head back, as if to shake off the thought.

Inside, the phone was ringing again. This time she answered without hesitation, knowing that it would be Tom. Once more the brief pause, the husbanding of strength.

"Sophie?"

How strange to hear her name in his voice. Five minutes earlier she couldn't have said with certainty that he knew she existed.

"Yes?"

"This is your father. Your father-in-law. Bill Crane. Tom's father."

The more he spoke, the more convinced she became that something was wrong with him.

"I know who you are."

"We haven't met," he said, as though she might doubt it. "I feel bad about that. I've wanted to meet you."

"Why are you calling?"

She didn't like taking this tone but felt bound to it.

"I'm at Saint Vincent's, recovering from some surgery. Minor stuff, exploratory. Supposed to let me out two hours ago. But one of the nurses gave me something for pain. Now they say they have to release me into someone's care."

Sophie took a moment with this news.

"I'm sorry to hear about that," she eventually said, which was true. "I hope you're all right."

"Sixty-two-year-old man, and they can't let me go without a chaperone."

"Did you try the number I gave you?"

"Tom wouldn't—that is, I couldn't get through to him. I just need someone to come down here and walk me outside, that's all. Maybe sign some kind of form. Once I'm out on the street I'll be fine."

"If you wait a few hours, I'm sure they'll let you go."

"I can't wait," he said. "I can't stay here."

She felt then his desperation's full force. The sound in his voice wasn't drink, or even whatever drugs they'd given him, but terror fighting to contain itself.

"Isn't there anyone else who can help?"

If there had been anyone else, he never would have called.

"Perhaps you should try Tom again later."

They both knew he'd already reached Tom, already been refused.

"I can't leave on my own until tomorrow, and I can't spend another night here."

She wasn't sure she wanted to help the man, wasn't even entirely sure that it was the right thing to do. The voice that urged her on, she recognized with some surprise, was one she hadn't heard for some time—not the voice of conscience, but the voice of curiosity. The voice that said, *It would make a great story.*

"I'll be there in half an hour."

In her first years with Tom, Sophie had often thought about meeting his father. She had worried over it, dreamed of it. A great deal of mystery had built up around him, mystery that Tom was not inclined to address, and so it was natural that she should be curious. But her interest went further: if there was a mystery she wished to solve in meeting Tom's father, it may have been Tom himself.

She hadn't thought at first that there was anything mysterious about him. He was just another of those boys who majored in economics and lived on the row, the boys she fell in with during her breaks from Charlie, boys who became temporarily enthralled, finding her unlike the other girls, but proved ready to move along as quickly as she was. It was senior year when he introduced himself, the second day of the fall recess. Though the dining hall was open, it was as empty as the rest of campus when she came in for lunch. She was sitting alone at one of the long rectangular tables, eating a salad in a large plastic bowl, when he set his tray down beside her.

"You're in my philosophy class," he said.

Indeed, she was. Introduction to Ontology.

"In a manner of speaking," she answered.

"How's that?"

"I mean, we may need to define our predicate more precisely."

He looked genially confused as he sat down.

"I don't really get it," he told her. "I'm just fulfilling my Lib Arts requirement."

"Ah, yes," she said. "Lib Arts. I'd forgotten about that requirement."

He didn't seem to know that she was being rude. He might just have been dumb, but she suspected—and he later admitted—that he'd been waiting some time to talk to her and wouldn't be put off by her sarcasm.

"So what are you doing here?" she asked, trying to be friendlier now, though it didn't come out that way.

He'd been given an extension on a paper, which he'd finished that morning. He was headed home in a few hours.

"How about you?"

After several years of spending breaks in New York with the Blakemans, she was back to having no place to go when campus shut down, since she wasn't speaking to Charlie. She didn't say this, of course. She just told him she was hanging around for the week.

"You could come with me, if you want," he said. "There's plenty of room at the family house, and we're always happy for visitors."

He seemed to speak without thinking. She was against character types in theory but found them useful practically, and she told herself that she knew this type. He had taken a chance on a spontaneous invitation that might get him lucky over the break. She preferred believing this to believing that an actual act of kindness was being extended. She didn't want to admit that right then she so badly needed a place for herself in the world that she would accept such kindness from a near stranger, but she could strike a more balanced deal.

His name, Tom O'Brien, was nearly all she knew of him, so she pictured a large Irish brood: garrulous raconteur father and smiling mother who played at being put upon though everyone understood she was really in charge, endless brothers and sisters and indistinguishable cousins, perhaps a set of twins somewhere among them, amid all of which the odd friend from school might easily be lost. On the drive down—home, it happened, was in southern Jersey, just a few hours from New Hampton—she asked about his family.

"Give me some notes," she said, "so I know who everyone is."

"Oh, it's just me and Beth."

"Beth?"

"My mother's sister, Beth O'Brien. She raised me."

"Your parents?" Sophie asked.

"Not around."

"Mine either," she said, suspecting he already knew as much. "Picnic, lightning."

"Excuse me?"

"Car crash," she explained. "Very literary. How about yours?"

"They died in a fire," Tom said. Or so Sophie would remember it. Perhaps he said they were "lost" or "taken" or some other construction that was honest in the strictest semantic sense, but he clearly suggested that both his parents had been killed. He'd taken the name O'Brien after coming to live with Beth at the age of eight. Another orphan, Sophie thought. As if absence created vacuums that pulled them to each other. It was, in retrospect, a very intimate conversation for two people who had more or less just met. But this was during a time when life seemed to Sophie a series of such intimacies, her losses extended like a hand to be shaken upon introduction.

"So it will be the three of us?"

"Is that all right?"

"I just hope I'm not intruding."

"Not at all. Like I told you, Beth loves visitors."

They stopped on the way to eat dinner, and it was late by the time they arrived at the small, two-story Queen Anne Victorian, one in a row of houses in similar style, with a wraparound porch and a tower along its right side that extended above the roof. The porch light was on, and Tom's aunt opened the door before they had finished pulling into the driveway. She was surprisingly beautiful, with pale skin and reddish blond hair that curled slightly toward her thin face. Only her outfit—a shapeless floral dress that ran to the ground—suggested the spinster aunt Sophie had been imagining for the last hour of their drive. When Tom introduced them, Beth took Sophie into a light but real embrace.

Tom and Beth led her to a small guest room on the first floor, where Sophie unpacked the few things she'd thrown together after lunch. She was anxious about spending the next week with strangers, and she didn't really understand their eagerness to take her in. There were shelves along one wall, and out of nervous habit she examined the books, one thing that could always give some comfort. She recognized few of the titles, most to do with religion, a topic about which Sophie knew almost nothing. *The Belief of Catholics*, *The Seven Storey Mountain*, *Guide to Aquinas*.

"How do you and Tom know each other?" Beth asked Sophie as Tom brought his things to his room.

She resisted the urge to say that they didn't.

"We take a philosophy course together," she answered instead.

"That's funny," Beth said. "I didn't know the subject interested Tom."

During the short tour of the house that followed, Beth caught Sophie looking at a framed photograph sitting on a side table, a picture of a smiling young woman—it might have been Beth herself—with an infant on her hip.

"That's my sister," Beth said. "Tom's mom. She died when Tom was young."

In the photograph, the woman stood alone with her child.

That night at Beth's house, Sophie waited for Tom to come down to her room. Driving her there and introducing her to what amounted to his family was more of an effort than most would make, and it seemed to entitle him to such a visit. If he comes, she thought, I'll do whatever he wants. As it was, he didn't come.

The next day Tom took Sophie into town, and they walked together along Main Street. Every few blocks a former teacher or the parent of an old classmate or a friend of Beth's stopped them on the street. Each one gave Tom a hug and asked how college was treating him.

"You must be almost done by now?"

"I graduate this spring," Tom said.

"And what's next?"

"I'm going to law school at Columbia."

"Sounds like you didn't do so hot at that college," joked Tom's high school baseball coach. Then he told Sophie what a star Tom had been on his team, their best pitcher, throwing a one-hit shutout in the county playoffs that people still talked about.

Was life really like this for anyone?

Sophie found herself happy for the first time in months, most of all because none of it had anything to do with her. This town was a place she couldn't have imagined for herself, that had existed all this time without her knowing about it. She was happy most of all because the world that welcomed her now gave no sign that it had been waiting for her, or that it would notice when she was gone.

Each night she prepared for him, as she prepared each day for an arm to find its way clumsily around her, or a hand to brush against her back. By the fourth night her surprise had turned to genuine disappointment. On the fifth night she went to him herself. He welcomed her, but anxiously, seeming only barely pleased. It took two more such nights before he settled himself, at which point she understood that all that week he had been terrified of her, terrified of his need for a girl he hardly knew. By then it was time to go back to campus. When she and Tom returned two months later to spend Christmas with Beth, they were a couple, and Sophie still believed Tom's father was dead.

She had never been inside St. Vincent's Hospital, though she'd walked by it many times. At the reception desk she asked for William Crane and was sent to an upper floor, where she asked again for him.

"I'm his daughter-in-law," she explained to a nurse behind the counter. "I'm here to pick him up."

The nurse's laugh seemed almost flirtatious.

"He's quite a handful," she said. "Tried to slip out on us twice. We nearly had to put him in restraints."

Sophie sat for a few minutes, until she felt a presence standing over her. When she looked up she found not the man she'd been expecting, some decaying echo of her husband, but a woman not much older than herself.

"Mrs. Crane?" the woman asked.

"Sophie," she said.

"I'm Dr. Phillips. I wondered, while I have you here, if we might talk."

Sophie expected to be taken into an office somewhere, but the doctor led her into an empty hospital room. It had been years since Sophie had been in one. The absence of patients gave it an eerie air, as if she and the doctor were conversing among the dead.

"Your father-in-law is quite upset that we've kept him here, I know. But really there wasn't any other way."

"I understand."

"How much do you know about his condition?"

"Not much," Sophie said. "To be honest, we've never met."

Dr. Phillips seemed relieved that she wasn't actually confronting a grieving loved one.

"It's quite serious."

"Is he dying?"

"Yes." Then she clarified. "There are still some things we can try, of course. We went in for an endoscopy, to take a look at some growths in his stomach. We found a substantial presence in some nearby lymph nodes. Possibly also his liver. We're going to know more after we get the results of his biopsy back, but it's not a great prognosis we're looking at. I think our most promising course is going to be a complete gastrectomy. That is, we'll take out his stomach. While we're in there, we can also take out those lymph nodes and some surrounding tissue."

She paused like a teacher measuring classroom comprehension.

"I'm sorry to be telling you all this in this way. We don't have a lot of choice. I've explained things to Mr. Crane, but he isn't in great shape, and I'm not sure how much he's taking in. I understand that he and your husband aren't close, but you're the only contacts he's given us."

"What exactly are you looking for us to do?"

"Well, there are ways to make all of this easier for him. Mr. Crane doesn't take very good care of himself. For starters, he doesn't seem to be taking his medicine. I'm going to write some scrips for you, and I want you to make sure he gets them filled."

"I can do that," Sophie said. "But I can't promise much else. My husband and his father don't get along."

The doctor was already handing over the prescriptions.

"Just do what you can. Ultimately, of course, he's responsible for his own well-being."

A duty had been discharged then, another imposed, and there was a subtle shift in balance between the two women as they walked out into the hall and back to the reception area.

"Here's my card," Dr. Phillips said by way of parting. "If you have any questions, you can call."

After she left, Sophie filled out the forms and waited for Crane's arrival.

Later, Sophie imagined that he had first appeared like a ghost, his pale green hospital gown emanating from him in waves. She imagined him floating toward her, bringing with him an obligation—as every spirit does—as though the demand he would eventually make was present in that instant, carried palpably within him.

But he was already dressed to leave, in a loose black T-shirt and black jeans, an outfit Sophie recognized as the uniform of a particular kind of older man who haunted lower Manhattan. He still wore his hospital slippers, shuffling to her, and if he resembled anything otherworldly, it was a creature from some medieval portrait of perdition, his pale face animated only by fear. The look made his obvious resemblance to Tom—square jaw; proud nose; thin, tight mouth—all the more troubling. His hair was white where it grew in patchy stubble on his cheeks and chin; it was gray and slight on top of his head, where it had been combed back in an effort to make him presentable. The nurse who walked beside him pointed him toward Sophie. Perhaps she knew, as the doctor seemed already to have known, that no real relationship existed between them.

"Mr. Crane," Sophie said, reaching out a hand to him.

He only nodded, and she dropped her hand back to her side. Neither spoke again until they were in the elevator.

"Thank you," he said. "I couldn't stay any longer."

His voice suggested little in the way of gratitude. But she didn't want gratitude. Better that he understand her arrival as an act of duty. This was how she wanted to understand it herself. She wanted to believe that she was behaving against her own will, if only so she could say as much to Tom. Yet letting the man spend one night in the hospital would not have weighed so heavily on her. She had come for herself. She had come to meet Tom's father.

"You can leave me here," he told her out on the street.

"I'm taking you home."

"You don't need to do that."

"I signed a form in there," she said, as though the form had anything to do with it. "I'm going to take you home and get your prescriptions filled. If you don't like it, I can bring you back upstairs."

She struggled to strike the right tone. She felt more sympathy than she'd expected she would, more than she wanted to feel, and overbearing authority from her would only make his situation more pathetic. But she didn't mean to budge, and she needed him to know it.

"I live on Fourth and C," he said. "The pharmacist is right up the block."

She helped him into a cab, and they rode in silence. There was everything still to say.

He untucked his shirt, reaching under it to bother at something in his gut. Some kind of surgical scar, she guessed. She thought, *So this is the man.* Tom hadn't wanted her to know Crane, would have been happy enough if she'd never learned that he existed, and it was difficult to shake the idea that an act of kindness toward one was a betrayal of the other. Or that Tom would think of it that way, which amounted to much the same thing. But everything she had seen thus far that day confirmed the secret image of Tom's father she'd kept these years, the image of a sad man who had made mistakes he didn't know how to redress, a man against whom hearts had been hardened. Such a man was owed kindness from those in the position to offer it.

They had his name on file at the drugstore, and the pharmacist told Sophie that the prescriptions would be ready in an hour and a half. They walked another block, and she followed him up the stairs to a three-room railroad apartment, the sort that many of her college friends had occupied in their first years out of school. There were papers everywhere, loose pages and newspaper clippings, some of them very old, by the looks of it. Most were collected into manila folders, as if to suggest organization, a gesture that only made the mess seem more desperate.

"Why don't you lie down," she told him, "and I'll pick up your drugs in a bit."

He nodded silently, still working through his shirt at whatever bothered him underneath. Then he disappeared into the bedroom, leaving her alone amid his ruins.

She had at least an hour, which she might have spent outside, in a diner or a café. Instead she created some space for herself on the couch by pushing one of the folders to the floor. For a moment, as she looked over the papers and general disarray, she thought: *This could be me. This could be my life.* She felt unaccountably exhausted.

When she stood she felt queasy, unstable on her feet. She went to the kitchen for a glass of water and found the sink overfull with dirty dishes, the cupboard empty. She washed and filled one glass. But before taking a sip she started cleaning the others.

Her own father, an investment advisor prey to wild shifts in mood, had never seemed happier than in the act of physical labor, raking leaves or chopping wood in their yard in Connecticut. He'd tried to instill this in her, often inviting her to join him in his work. Now, when she spent a day sweeping and vacuuming, she thought of him. Or didn't think of him, exactly, for the fact of not thinking accounted for a good deal of the pleasure those days provided. But her unthinking self, her brute body at work, felt close to her father then, and she liked the work for this reason.

She didn't care much for washing dishes, though. It kept you fixed in one place and didn't have the feel of true labor. On the rare occasions when Tom was home in time for dinner, Sophie made him clean up afterward. But now the warm water comforted her hands. The one dishtowel was dirtier than most of the dishes, but there was soap and a dish rack, and she had enough to make do. Once she'd finished, she took her glass into the living room. There too, she tidied up. When she handled Crane's folders, the urge was great to look through them. But Sophie resisted, sensing where that would lead, the entanglement that such interest would bring. She straightened them into piles neat enough to suggest at least the possibility of order. She thought she might buy cleaning supplies while at the drugstore, so she could do a proper job when she got back.

It occurred to her to check on Crane before going to fill his prescriptions, but she wanted to let him sleep. She was there and back before she realized that she hadn't taken a key. She buzzed his apartment twice, knowing that he would sleep through it, before moving on to others. A voice with a heavy Spanish accent came over the intercom.

"Hello?"

"Oh, I'm sorry," Sophie said. "I'm running an errand for the man on the fourth floor, and I've been locked out."

The intercom went dead, and a woman emerged from a first-floor apartment and trundled down the hall.

"You're running errands for Mr. Crane?" the woman asked, holding the building's front door open a few unwelcoming inches. She was short and overstuffed, in her fifties perhaps, with black hair and questioning eyes.

"I just stepped out for a moment, but I forgot the key."

"Mr. Crane doesn't get visitors. We live here both ten years, and he never get a visitor."

"I'm his daughter," she said, which seemed near enough to true and likely to carry some force.

"He never mentioned having children. You're his daughter, and you don't visit all these years?"

"I'm sorry," Sophie said, unsure for what. Then she showed the woman the bag from the pharmacy, pointing to the prescription label. "See here, William Crane, it says."

Perhaps this suggested something official, for the woman now spoke with deference. "I'm Lucia Ortiz."

"Nice to meet you, Ms. Ortiz. I'm Sophie."

"Mr. Crane is sick? I live with him a very long time. He's a very nice man. He's quiet, but very nice."

Sophie felt the introduction of this woman into her story as an act of providence—as, in truth, she was inclined to treat all such introductions—and she saw at once how she was meant to make use of it.

"Yes, I'm afraid he's quite sick." She gestured at the bag of pill bottles, now in Lucia's hands. "Do you think you could bring those to him later, so I don't have to disturb him while he sleeps?"

"That's no problem," said Lucia Ortiz, obviously relieved not to have to let Sophie into the building.

"Another thing." Sophie hesitated. "If you have a chance, could you just check in on him once in a while? I'm going to try to see him soon, but it's hard for me. I'll leave a number you can call if anything happens."

Sophie wrote her name and her cell phone number on a piece of paper she found in her purse. She took out a twenty-dollar bill and awkwardly handed it to Lucia along with the paper.

"No, no," Lucia told her, returning the bill. She gestured to the cross around Sophie's neck, almost touching it. "God's blessing to you, Sophie Crane. I'll look in on your father."

As Sophie entered her apartment she heard the phone ringing, and she had the unsettling feeling that it was morning again. She was coming back from mass, and she would have to live the entire exhausting day over again. This time she didn't wait to pick up. She wanted to get it all over with.

"Hello?"

"You answered."

How happy she was to hear her husband's voice, to find it unchanged by what she'd done.

"Are you coming home soon?"

"I wish you would have picked up earlier. I've been calling for hours."

"I'm sorry," she said. "I was out. You should have called my cell."

"It's been turned off all day."

"I'm sorry," she said again.

"What have you been up to?" She sensed him trying to calm himself, waiting for her to confirm his fears.

"I went to get your father from the hospital."

As she said this, it might have been just another chore that they'd both known she had to fulfill, as it would in another family.

"Soph."

"I had no choice, Tom. The man is old and very sick and alone."

"It's his own fault he's alone."

She wanted to tell him how it felt in Crane's apartment, wanted to say that she saw there all the things that he had saved her from. More than that, she wanted him to want to hear about his father.

"Maybe so," she finally said.

"And if he didn't need something from us, he never would have called."

"That's probably true."

In the quiet that followed, certain ideas burst forth that she guarded carefully. He had a parent, as she did not, and it was inhuman of him to forsake this legacy, no matter what the man had done.

"Let's not do this now," she said. "We can talk when you get home."

"I'm going to be held up here for a while."

"Okay. I'll try to wait up. If I can't, I'll make us a big breakfast and we'll talk in the morning."

"All right."

"Don't be mad."

"I'll get over it," he said.

"I love you," she told him.

"You too, kid."

A moment before she would have liked to talk with him forever. Now she hung up the phone in relief.

3

LONG AFTER WANDERING upstairs that night, I heard the laughter and talk on the floor below. We'd always let those parties run their natural course, and I had learned to sleep amid that murmur, like one who lives near the sea. But on that night I stayed up, listening to the noise downstairs, trying to make out Sophie's voice. I had waited about an hour downstairs before giving up on her return, and I still couldn't sleep without knowing if she'd come back. By my best estimate, it had been a year since I'd seen Sophie, at the wedding of a New Hampton friend. Now that we had been returned to each other, I didn't want her to disappear again. She came in finally to say good night, stepping through a sheet of dusty light in the doorway, as though she knew I'd been waiting for her.

"Sleep," she said, when I sat up to reach for her. "In the morning, we can talk."

But the uneasiness didn't pass once she was gone. I realized that I had known all along that she would find a couch or one of the spare beds when the party wound down, that

I would see her in the morning. I had been listening for her not because I doubted her return, but because I wanted to know she wasn't with Max.

Max was a sophomore at Yale the year Sophie and I started college. Early in December, he took the train down to visit me. Two of his high school friends went to New Hampton, and the three of them took me out that weekend. It was typical that Max should show me around my own campus. Though he was only a year older, I had always followed his lead.

I hadn't socialized much in the first two months of the semester. Each Friday afternoon I'd ridden New Jersey Transit into Penn Station to spend the weekend with my mother. She insisted it wasn't necessary, but I didn't feel right going out with friends while she stayed at home so soon after my father's death. His illness had been a slow process of subtraction—his hair was taken, his strength, his teeth, his mind—so that it was hard to say exactly what was lost on that day a few weeks before my graduation from St. Albert's when the last of him went. Yet nothing that came before had prepared us for it. It may be that whatever remained of his consciousness was relieved to have it end, but I wanted only for him to still be there, even in all his suffering.

When my father was alive, we'd eaten at the table in the dining room, but now it seemed too big for us. My mother would make dinner on Friday night, and we would sit on stools at the kitchen counter while we ate. Each weekend I arrived with the hope of being a comfort, but once I was with her I found it impossible. I suppose I wanted her to comfort me, though I knew that this too was impossible. She asked about my classes, but there wasn't much to say, since I wasn't going to most of them, having discovered that I could get away with doing almost no work at New Hampton. I had already decided never to submit to the rituals of job interviews and grad school applications, so grades meant little to me. I only needed to pass so I could take my fiction workshop. I stayed in my room, writing stories or reading the books that Sophie mentioned on our walks back from class, while my textbooks sat untouched.

After we'd exhausted my academic life as a topic of discussion, my mother would ask about my classmates and my social life. It was Friday night and I was eating dinner with my mother an hour away from campus—that was my social life. Sophie was the only person I'd met who mattered to me, and I was somehow unable even to mention her name.

My mother was still working, ostensibly at least, as a real estate agent, but she had stopped picking up listings while taking care of my father, and she was struggling to get back to it. I wanted to learn how she was doing, but I didn't know where to begin such a conversation. "What fills your days?" I might have asked, but who asks such a thing? What answer could she have given that I was prepared to hear? My presence did nothing for her suffering except embarrass it with an audience.

An open bottle of wine sat on the counter between us each night. I generally drank a glass or two while my mother drank the rest. Sometimes I drank more, so that there would be less left for her, but this approach had its own risks. If I took too much from the bottle, she would open another. After dinner, we went to her room, where we climbed into bed together and watched reruns until she fell asleep. She woke when I turned off the TV, so I learned to leave it on, lowering the volume a bit before creeping to the door and dimming the lights. Then I headed down the hall with a sour taste in my mouth to spend the rest of the weekend as I would have had I been at school—alone in my room. By the time I left, we both felt a bit worse than we had upon my arrival, and I told myself that I would stay on campus from then on. But when Friday came around again, I went back to New York.

This continued until Thanksgiving, which we spent with Max and his parents at their apartment. After that, I stayed three days in my room, working on a short story whose details I have since entirely forgotten.

"You need to have a normal life at school," my mother said that Sunday before sending me off for my train. "Why don't you stay down there next weekend?"

"I don't mind," I told her. "I can come back up."

"Charlie," she said, her tone soft but insistent. "I don't want you to come back up."

On campus I discovered that my classmates had been working tirelessly. Unlike course work, constructing a social life required sustained attention. You couldn't hang around one Saturday out of three or four and expect to follow along with others who had been doing all the reading and taking all the notes. My roommate, Dean, a friendly but somewhat awkward kid from Cleveland who had not struck me as a social adept, invited me to a party in another freshman's room. When it finished, I followed him to the fraternity houses.

"Do you have any blues?" he asked as we stood in a line outside a Tudor-style mansion filled with drunk kids.

"What's that?"

"Jesus, man," Dean said. "You can't get in the door without a pass. They rotate the colors. Tonight it's blue."

"No, I don't have any blues."

"I'd like to help you out," he said. "But I've been hustling all week to get three passes, and I told this cute girl from Orgo that I'd get her and her roommate in."

Dean looked at me as though I had presented him with a serious ethical dilemma.

"No big deal," I said. "It's just a party."

So I passed the balance of another night reading alone in my room.

This all changed when Max arrived the next weekend. Like Dean, he took me to a room party, but this one was in an upper-class dorm, where we drank beer from a half keg lodged behind two couches in case of an inspection by the campus police. Max reintroduced me to his old friends, two guys I'd known vaguely at St. Albert's. When the crowd started to thin, we sat in a circle getting stoned from a six-inch plastic water pipe.

"Charlie, man," one of Max's friends said. "I knew you were here, but I never see you. We need to hang out."

"I've been working a lot lately," I said. "But I'm starting to go out more. I mean, yeah, we should do something."

As we walked out to the fraternity houses, I realized that I didn't have any passes, didn't even know what colors would be accepted. But the issue never came up. We walked to the front of a line stretching off the porch onto the manicured lawn and were ushered inside. I had found my way into a few of the houses by then, but none of the more popular ones, which seemed to serve some related but separate population.

We were in the basement, standing near a Ping-Pong table, when I felt the tap on my shoulder. Before I could turn around, Sophie had wrapped her arms around my neck and kissed me on the cheek. "You're here!" she said, as if it were a great shock that I should be out with everyone else. Which to me it was, though I wouldn't have expected her to notice it. We'd walked back from class each week for a month, but otherwise we hadn't spoken much. Now I was stoned and she was drunk, and for a moment we stood stupidly regarding each other. I tried not to be disappointed at how well she fit in with the others, how wholly comfortable she looked among them. She seemed to be thinking the same about me. I wanted to explain that it wasn't so. Max introduced himself and his friends, and Sophie introduced the girls who stood beside her. A few minutes of conversation passed, the kind of empty talk such situations demand, at which Max has always excelled. All the while Sophie and I looked at each other as if to say, We aren't really like this, are we?

"What's her story?" Max asked, when we were alone again.

"Just a girl from my writing class."

When I woke the next morning, I didn't remember much of the night, but I knew that I'd wandered back to my room alone. I was surprised to find Max asleep on the couch.

"How was the rest of your evening?" I asked when he rose to find me reading and smoking out the window.

"We did important work," he said. "It might have come too late for our own benefit, but future generations will thank us." He picked a crumb of dry drool from his stubbled cheek and regarded it scientifically. "The most important part is no one got hurt."

I laughed grimly. "You make any new friends?"

"You may have to be more specific," he said. "They're all friends, really. I am for those who believe in loose delights. I dance with the drinkers and drink with the dancers. Or something like that."

"You seemed to be after one delight, in particular."

Now he laughed. "The confusions of young Charlie."

"What do you mean by that?"

He threw off his blanket and got up from the couch, wearing only his boxer shorts. He looked around the room for his jeans, which he pulled on before taking a cigarette from their back pocket.

"How well do you know that girl Sophie?"

"Like I said last night, she's in my writing class. Why?"

"Well, good luck and all. As far as I can tell, she's a dyke."

He sat back down on the couch and recounted the rest of his night to me. I'd left the basement angrily and without explanation—once he said it, this sounded plausible enough—and he and his friends had stayed out. They'd resumed talking to Sophie and the other girls, and when the house went off tap, they'd all gone back to campus to smoke pot and listen to music.

"Not sure whose room it was," Max said.

He'd hoped to hook up with Sophie, he admitted, but he wasn't sure how to play things without a place to take her.

"So at some point, I sort of lost my shit for a second. Seemed like a second to me, but I guess it was longer, because I come to, and the music is still playing, but I'm the only one in the room, and I'm very stoned. I figure I should head back here, but I thought I'd look around a little first. Do not go gently, and all. So I give a knock on one of the bedroom doors, and I hear some rustling inside. I go ahead in, and your friend and one of the other girls are there in bed together."

"So they went to sleep in the same bed. Girls do that."

"So they do. And in support of your theory, the other girl was still wearing all her clothes. But Sophie was most of the way toward bare. I wouldn't quite say they were *in flagrante*, but they weren't exactly *ex flagrante*, either. At any rate, it's a good thing we didn't come to blows over her last night, which is where you looked to be headed, because the winner would have had a catfight on his hands."

"I think you might be experiencing a bit of psychic leakage," I told him. "Or maybe just wish fulfillment."

"The boy is incredulous. I guess they don't teach Plato at this school. The sexes are three, because the sun, moon, and earth are three." He dropped his cigarette into an empty beer can at his feet and went in search of a T-shirt. "Come on," he said. "Buy me some brunch and I'll tell you all about the birds and the bees."

I hadn't realized before Max's visit how much this girl, about whom I really knew nothing, had taken over my thoughts. But the realization came just as the hope of acting on it was closed off. I was angry without knowing why, my anger both unjustifiable and out of my control, and so I kept to myself for several days. I didn't go to workshop that week. Only when the afternoon arrived at the point when we might have been walking back to campus together did I regret the decision. I couldn't wait another week to talk to her.

When I heard the knock half an hour after the end of class, I opened the door with a mixture of panic and relief. She presented herself to me as if I'd been expecting her. Which, I suddenly felt, I had. She walked past me into the room, heading right for a poster on my wall of a model in a bikini, drinking a bottle of beer.

"I like it," she said after a moment of consideration. "It adds a quiet dignity."

"My roommate put it up. She belongs to him."

"Too bad." She leaned over and picked up the book I'd set on the floor when she knocked. "Perhaps you can work out a swap, one half-read copy of *Within a Budding Grove* for one young girl in flower."

"Seems like a fair trade."

She sat down on the windowsill where I'd been perched reading before her arrival, and I took a place on the couch.

"We missed you in class," she said, still holding my book. "It's dreadful being literary without someone there to appreciate it."

"I was falling behind on my education."

"You should have started with Nabokov. He's a bit more concise."

"I did."

"Really, which one?"

"*Pale Fire. Ada.* A few of the early Russian novels."

She seemed pleased but embarrassed to learn I'd been following her reading course, and she turned away to set down the volume of Proust.

"Have you gotten far enough to know the truth about Albertine?"

"There have been hints," I said. "But the narrator seems a bit obtuse."

"Maybe I can offer some insight, then."

Of insight, Sophie had plenty. She had been a senior in high school when her parents were killed in a car crash while driving home from a party just a few miles from their house. She told me this as if describing the plot of an unconvincing book she'd been forced to read for class. She'd already been accepted by New Hampton at the time, but both the admissions office there and her high school counselor urged her to defer for a year. They must have assumed that she would spend that time with family, but she had no family to speak of. Since she was already eighteen—

"I'd reached my majority," she told me, in a faux-clinical voice—she was free to live by herself in her parents' house. She wrote for days on end. When she wasn't writing, she haunted the local bookstore, run by a woman in her thirties who'd dropped out of grad school to take over the store when her parents, the owners, retired. The woman's name was Lila. She gave Sophie a reading list, and they conducted a kind of seminar together.

"Now here's the sordid, predictable part," Sophie told me. "It wasn't just a literary education I received. If a certain kind of author were telling the story, we would turn the sign on the door from 'open' to 'closed' and fall into passion right there at the foot of the shelves. It wasn't quite like that. But close enough."

By the time the next fall came around, Sophie was ready to give up on college entirely. But a few weeks into the semester, Lila decided she didn't want Sophie's future on her conscience.

"I was completely in love with her. She told me I could stay at home or come here, whichever was right for me, but either way things were through between us. I've called her a few times since I got here. She chats politely, but she doesn't want to give me ideas. To be honest, I'm not really sure that I like girls. I know that I like her, but she won't have me."

What little I already knew about Sophie—that she wrote better than the rest of us, that she had read more and better books, that she was somehow not of this place—now made sense. I pictured her alone in her parents' empty house, writing that long story I'd read a few weeks before. It didn't diminish what she'd done, but it made it fathomable.

There wasn't anything I could say in response, so I told her the first thing that came to mind.

"My father died six months ago."

I'd been hesitant before then to speak to people at school about his death. I didn't know what others would make of it. In truth, I didn't yet know what to make of it myself. I wasn't quite a child then, and so not quite a tragic case, but my loss was still an occasion for pity, which may have been what kept me from discussing it. I also had a vague sense that something of such importance would be cheapened by casual talk, becoming the thing that defined me in the superficial way that others were defined by the sport they played or the music they liked. But now that I had the chance to make myself known to Sophie, this was the first thing I mentioned.

She only nodded in response, as if to say: I know he did; that's why I found you.

And perhaps she did know. It was a small campus, where word spread around. At the very least, Max's friends would have already known. Or she might have heard something from Max himself. It was just the kind of thing one brought up, stoned and sentimental, at the end of such a night. I never asked her what she already knew about me when she came to my room that day. But before then we hadn't spoken at length about anything other than books, and now we each seemed desperate to be understood by the other.

The next week, I invited her to come to New York over winter break. My mother and I were both relieved to have someone else in the house, and Sophie seemed glad to have someplace to go. She came with us to midnight mass on Christmas Eve, an old family tradition that had largely been my father's doing, which we were enacting without him for the first time. We ate Christmas dinner at my aunt and uncle's house, and Max introduced Sophie to his parents as though she had come as his guest.

He liked to remind me in later years that my entire relationship with Sophie might never have happened without his visit. He did this playfully, but there was a point to it. He was saying that I had no special claim over her.

I expected the usual morning-after mess when I went downstairs, but Gerhard's living room was empty and clean, the windows open to let in car horns and breeze. The place looked less like the house that Max and I occupied than like its owner's best hopes for that house when he left it in our care. Sophie walked out of the kitchen with a dust pan and a broom.

"You didn't have to do all this," I said.

"It's no trouble," she answered. "I like housework. Except the dishes. I left those for you."

Her hair was pinned up so that from the front she looked as she used to when she'd worn it short. Her outfit too, tight black jeans and a black T-shirt, reminded me of those days.

"You've changed."

She laughed uncomfortably.

"The ravages of time."

"Your clothes, I meant."

Again she laughed, more freely, and she looked down at herself in feigned surprise.

"I did some shopping after mass this morning. Max tells me there's an empty room, if you don't mind my staying for a while." Before I could respond she added, "Come have a seat. I just put some coffee on."

"I have to walk the dog," I said.

So it was that Sophie and I followed Ginger through Washington Square as a bright autumn morning neared noon.

"You published your novel," she said.

"I did."

"Congratulations. I'm sorry, I should have told you that a lot sooner."

"That's all right. It's not very good."

"No," she said. "Not really."

"You read it?"

"Of course I read it."

When the book appeared the previous spring, I'd expected some word from Sophie, and her silence had been a sad reminder of our falling-out. Over time, it grew to become the single big disappointment that stood in for the many small disappointments surrounding the book's failure, as if it all finally amounted to the absence of the one reader whose opinion mattered. Which it did: I'd been writing all along to her. I knew that what I'd done wasn't worth much, but I was ready to do something more. My great difficulty in getting started again—or so I had told myself—was the realization that she wasn't listening.

"Anyway, it was a start," I said. "I'll do better with the follow-up."

"You're precocious. It takes most writers years to regret their first book."

I didn't need to tell her that I'd read the story collection she'd published the year after we graduated, the book that had briefly given her the literary fame that Max so badly wanted for us. Sophie and I had still been close when she wrote those stories, and I'd been the first to read them.

"How's your own follow-up going?" I asked.

"It's finished."

"That's great," I said. "When can I read it?"

"It's not that kind of finished. No one's going to read it."

"Have you shown it to your editor?" I asked.

Sophie waved at the air in front of us, swatting away in one go my question and her book. She'd never been the kind to disparage her work for form's sake or to elicit some empty reassurances. She'd never made a drama of it, never declared at the end of a bad day, It's all shit; I'm giving up. If she said she was through with her novel, she meant it.

Near the fountain, a crowd was gathering around three teenagers who were break-dancing to eighties hip-hop. Sophie and I stood on its outskirts, half watching the boys.

"Last week," I said, "I bought my high school yearbook off the street."

"Sounds promising," she said. "Tell me more."

"It was on Sixth Avenue, near the Jefferson Market library. I walked by one of those guys selling used books on the sidewalk. Leon Uris and Erica Jong. Fifteen-year-old issues of *Glamour*. You wonder where they get all this shit. And there was my yearbook. St. Albert's, class of '92."

In fact, the yearbook had been from the class ahead of mine—Max's class—and I'd found it months before. But I wanted to tell her a story, the way we had always done, and this was the first that came to mind.

"I stopped and opened it up to look at the inscriptions. It had belonged to a guy named Justin. He was a scholarship kid, I remember, transferred from public school around sixth or seventh grade. I'd known him pretty well. I mean, we weren't close or anything, but it was a small school. We all knew each other. I guess he threw the yearbook out after graduation, or gave it away, or sold it with a bunch of old textbooks or something."

"Had you written anything in it?" Sophie asked.

"Sure," I answered, as if to say, *If that's what you want to have happened.* "I wrote, 'To Justin—Your secret is safe with me.'"

In better days, this is where Sophie and I would have begun spinning a plot out together, trying to outdo each other or leading the tale through baroque digressions and leaving the other to bring it back out. I had given her an easy opening, and now I watched her struggle to do something with it, disappointed that we couldn't fall more easily into old habits. We were both out of practice, but this was more than that. She looked exhausted.

"So, I bought the thing," I said eventually. "It was two or three bucks. I thought I'd track Justin down, find out what he's up to, and give the book back to him."

"But you won't," Sophie said.

"No, I won't."

"You don't want to hear the ending."

"Because the story's too good."

During our freshman spring, when we'd been close for only a few months but already felt certain that our lives were bound together, Sophie told me about a habit of the young Henry James. Probably Lila had told her first. During his early years in London, James went out to dinner parties every night and listened while the other guests talked. When someone started a story that sounded promising, that gave him a *donnée*, as he called those initial germs of his books, James would ask the speaker to stop. If he knew how the story turned out, all its potential would be spoiled for him. I thought she was suggesting some connection between the two of us and the seemingly feckless young man who would become the Master on whom nothing was lost.

"If he ever did that to me," Sophie said, "I'd tell him to fuck off. It's my story, Hank."

This was on one of those long nights we spent in Sophie's room, chain-smoking Camels and drinking Jameson. She called the whiskey "my Irish," which was an old line from her father. Perhaps because of her family situation, Sophie had been given a single room, a rarity for freshmen, and by that point I had more or less moved in. We shared the same bed, though this meant different things at different times. So much of our ardor was spent on talk and drink that we were often exhausted by the time we ended the night beside each other. At other times, we fell into fucking as though it were a conversation; it mattered, of course, but so did everything else we did together.

In the morning we'd wake up hungover and write while the rest of the world went off to class. We could spend hours just a few feet apart without saying a word. After lunch, we went walking.

Speaking again of his days in London, of walking home each night from an evening out, James described one of his novels as "the ripe round fruit of perambulation." Our relationship was that, I think. It began with walks back from class, but it developed in those long spring afternoons, when we meandered off campus through the surrounding town of New Hampton.

It was then that we initiated the game of telling stories together. One of us might look at an old woman and a younger man walking down the street together and say, "Everyone thinks she's my mother, that's the hardest part about falling in love." Half an hour later we'd have outlined an entire relationship. One or the other or both of us might eventually try to write something down about it, but that wasn't really the point. The point was that there were stories everywhere, waiting to be discovered by invention.

When I was young I played a solitary game: I closed my eyes and counted steps while walking down the street. After one or two, I still sensed exactly where I stood in relation to the world. At three I became uncomfortable, and by four or five I opened my eyes with great relief to discover familiarity all around me, to see that I could have gone on for many more steps. But it was too late; I could only start over. That is how my writing went before I met Sophie, beginning with great excitement and hopefulness that survived for a page or two despite growing disorientation. By page six I would open my eyes in the fear that I had become completely lost. It was on those walks, telling those stories, that I learned how to keep my eyes closed, how to give up this world and live in another long enough to make it seem real.

After we tired of telling stories, we talked about whatever we'd been reading that morning—a John Hawkes novel, a long poem by Merrill or Stevens. We spoke of them as she had spoken to me about the Beats and Nabokov on our first walk together, as we imagined those writers would have spoken about each other. Alfred Kazin once said of Saul Bellow that he was the first person he'd met who spoke of Lawrence and Hemingway not as idols but as competitors. This is how we tried to speak. We didn't pretend to be the equals of the writers we loved, but we were all in the same trade. Sometimes too we spoke about our classes, but only to disparage them.

"They wanted to talk about what we *learned* from Keats," Sophie said. "It's like asking what you learn from getting laid. I learned that I like how he makes me feel."

We walked until we were exhausted, and then we sat down on the sidewalk to rest before walking back to campus. Around this time, we both read the essay in which Thoreau offers the French *sans terre* as a root for the verb "to saunter." A true saunterer, he said, is without a land of his own. Our own wandering had in it that element of homelessness. There was something desperate to the way we walked, just as there was something desperate to the way we read and wrote, to the way we drank and smoked when we finally found our way back to her room.

During another of our late-night sessions, she mentioned that the semifamous visiting novelist who'd taught our workshop in the fall had kissed her during office hours. He was gone from campus by the time she told me, and he wanted her to visit him in New York.

"Are you going?" I asked.

She took a long sip of her Irish and her face puckered into itself. She shook it out. "It would make a great story," she said.

This had become a refrain between us, and at different times it meant different things. We spoke about our own lives almost exclusively as material, as a rough draft in which one learned what would work on the page. If Sophie thought that taking the train to New York was the best way to make a story out of our professor's proposition, then that's what she would do. But the expression also suggested the opposite: that stories could free us from experience, allowing us to spend days at a time silently near each other without feeling we were missing the world outside. If you could imagine a story into life, then you didn't need to live it. So her reply said nothing, really, about her intentions.

No one went on dates at New Hampton, but any couple that was sleeping together with some amount of exclusivity was said to be dating. In that sense, the term applied as well to us as to anyone. In the eyes of our friends, Sophie and I had been dating for several months. But she still spoke to me about Lila, and she still made occasional efforts to remind me that nothing between us was fixed. Whatever else it was, talk of our professor's invitation was another of these reminders.

Another story she liked to tell, handed down from Lila, involved Edmund Wilson and Edna St. Vincent Millay, who had been a classmate of Wilson's sister at Vassar. After Wilson discovered her work in an undergraduate anthology and helped to make her name in New York, Millay became the great bohemian beauty. Everyone fell in love with her, Wilson most of all. One day on the back porch of the Millay family home the age's greatest critic took a knee and proposed to her. After considering for a second she said, "I suppose that might solve it." She had assumed that he was offering a kindness, a convenient sheen of respectability beneath which she might go on writing her poems and sleeping with men and women as she liked. But Wilson meant only to make her his wife.

When the school year ended, I went back to my mother's apartment and Sophie went back to that big empty house in Connecticut. She hoped to spend the summer with Lila at the bookstore, but she returned to find the store closed. Lila responded to her e-mail after a few days, saying that she was traveling through Europe, sharpening up her languages before giving graduate school another shot. Sophie told me all this during one of her few visits to New York that summer. She didn't suggest that the end of her hopes with Lila meant anything one way or another for our own relationship. She stayed for the day, ate dinner with me and my mother, and got on the train back home.

If my father had still been alive, he would have made me work that summer. But he was gone, and my mother, busy again selling real estate, was happy to let me come and go as I pleased. I spent most of the summer reading and writing, thinking of Sophie doing the same up in Connecticut,

and feeling as though we were together. The stars, says
Thoreau, are the apexes of what wonderful triangles.

Back on campus in the fall, everything picked up just as
it had been. We both had single rooms now, but it was always her room where we spent those long days and nights,
drinking and talking and reading. We were supposed to
have chosen our classes before getting back, but Sophie
hadn't filled out the forms, and she asked me what I was
taking. She signed up for the ancient history survey and the
philosophy class I'd picked, but she shook her head over
the one course that had seemed obvious to me.

"Those workshops are pointless," she said.

And so we gave up our writing classes, though they were
the reason we'd both come to New Hampton in the first
place. From then on we showed our work only to each other.

Sophie returned to campus with a pile of short stories,
perhaps a dozen of them. One was "Visiting Professor,"
which would eventually become the title of her collection.
The narrator of the story is a college student who goes to
New York for a romantic dinner with an older professor
she idolizes. She knows that the man wants to sleep with
her, and she welcomes it. But outside the classroom he
lacks all the charm and self-assurance that had attracted
her. He gets drunk and cries embarrassingly over his wife,
who has left him. The narrator comforts him. The apartment he's been living in since his wife threw him out re-
minds her of a dozen dorm rooms she's been brought to
on other late nights, but she decides to stay there with him
anyway. When they get to his bedroom he's too drunk to
do anything but take a feeble swing at her and tell her to
leave. On the story's last page, the narrator sits in Penn
Station, waiting for the train back to New Jersey, thinking
of the boy she loves back on campus. She imagines how

she'll describe the evening to him, wondering what kind of story she wants it to be, whether to make it a comedy or a tragedy or some mixture of both.

Between the night when she told me about the kiss in the office and the day she gave me those thirty pages, she had never mentioned our actual professor. I didn't know if she had gone to see him or if the entire thing was invented. After reading the story, I couldn't ask. Not just because I didn't want to admit to being jealous, but because the story made the truth irrelevant. The telling was what mattered. So at least we believed then. I think now that we were wrong. What really happened does matter, even if we can only ever know it once it's too late to do anything about it.

Essentially everything that would wind up in her collection—a collection that won prizes, that "announced the debut of a great American writer," as the visiting professor himself put it on the book's dust jacket—was written during that time. My own work was strong enough, for undergraduate writing. But the decision to drop out of workshop was in part a declaration that we judged ourselves by other standards. By those higher standards, I was still lacking. It was something we both acknowledged without any particular discomfort: she was simply better than I was. But I was improving, writing with her in mind, knowing she wouldn't let me get away with anything. And we had all the time we needed. We never doubted that we would both make it. It had to happen, because we wanted it so badly. The certainty of that wanting left us free to ignore everything else around us, to give ourselves entirely.

I miss that about those days—the freedom to want; the belief that our desires could never disappoint us, so long as we remained loyal to them; the sense that we could choose our fate, as though the absence of choice weren't exactly what made it fate.

For all that, I shouldn't make it sound as though we spent three years in a hothouse together. In most ways, we lived like everyone on campus. At meals we sat with our classmates and had predictable dining hall conversations. We went to class when the spirit moved us and during those points in the year when it became unavoidable if one wanted to pass. On sunny days near the beginning and end of each school year we joined the world out in the courtyard, lying on blankets in the shade of our fake-Gothic dormitory, taking surreptitious sips from cans of warm beer. On weekends we sometimes went drinking with everyone else. But when Monday morning came, we began the week together, reading and writing on Sophie's couch, and days passed when we hardly spoke to anyone else.

Every few months, she closed her door to me. She might look up casually from a novel she was reading and ask, "Don't you think you ought to leave?" Or else, at the end of our usual walk she would announce that she was returning to her room in a tone that made clear I wasn't invited back with her. The first few times this happened, I asked if I'd done something wrong. She looked at me as though I was being ridiculous. Was it really so strange for her to want a bit of time to herself? Of course it wasn't, but it wasn't the deal I thought we had worked out.

Eventually, I came to see these breaks—the shortest a few days, the longest a few weeks—as part of the rhythm of time. They even brought some relief. Once away from her, I realized how constricting our life together could be. And yet I fell eagerly back into that life as soon as she was ready for me.

In the meantime, there were certain rules I came to understand. After she shut me out, I couldn't go to her. I had to wait for her to come to me, which she eventually did, usually in the middle of the night. She'd wake me gently, and then I would find her on top of me.

I knew she slept with other guys during our time apart. They were blond, sunny, unserious boys, business majors and players of squash. They seemed good-natured but perplexed by her sudden attention. She never made any attempt to conceal them from me, which would have been impossible at a school that size. Impossible, too, to avoid running into each other. I could be sure of seeing her every few days, walking to class with a group of other girls or even with the boy she was briefly trying out. She would wave or smile as if I were just another friend, and the latest boy, who knew that Sophie and I had been "together" in some amorphous way, would duck his head deferentially.

What I felt then wasn't as simple as jealousy. She lost focus for me. I saw her through the eyes of those others, for whom she was a figure of comic caprice or just an average girl. Worse, I felt myself come out of focus when I didn't have her attention. It wasn't just my writing but my entire life that I had come to compose with one reader in mind.

As we crossed Washington Square all those years later, back to our walking ways, we both came into focus again. I had the idea that we might be on the edge of a new life together, as though the past few years had been one of those regular interludes, and her marriage to Tom just another fling with a boy she'd picked out from nowhere. The crowd around the break-dancers had grown to include us, and Ginger ran tight circles around my legs, wrapping me in her leash as in a trap.

"You can have it if you want," I told Sophie. We were speaking still of the yearbook, but I meant the idea of it, the germ it represented. "I haven't been able to make it into much."

"I'm done with all that," she said. "Not just the novel." She seemed surprised to have to say as much, as though I should have known from looking at her. Perhaps I should have; I noticed again how tired she seemed, how much at a loss. "I gave up."

Had this been a recent decision, perhaps related to the end of her marriage, or had she given up long before? I could have asked, but I didn't. The Sophie who had existed all these years, her life running parallel to mine though out of sight, the one to whom I'd all along been sending secret messages I'd understood somehow were being received and even answered, that Sophie was still committed to our grand project. It didn't seem possible that she'd abandoned it without my knowing. So I chose to believe that she'd given up only recently, that she'd come to me for help on account of it.

4

SOMETIMES SHE WOKE too quickly, on the cusp of morning, before the world was ready for her. Then she would hear a hum in the distance that an untrained ear might mistake for falling rain or the labor of the air conditioner but which she knew for what it was: the sound of all the elements that make up a life, floating free of their proper place, awaiting the call to cohere. In that moment, before these parts had responded to her arrival, it was possible still for some new past to coalesce behind her, some new future to fix itself ahead, some other life to take her in its grip.

When Tom was there, his restless snore blew everything back into the shape of the one life to which she belonged, rather than one of the many to which she might have belonged and did not. But when he traveled for work there was only that hum, and the possibilities lingered.

This time, Tom stirred at her side. He opened his eyes to the half-darkened room and his wife sitting straight up in bed.

"Dreams?" he asked, giving the word a worried lilt. He was handsome now in the darkness.

"Dreams," she answered, and they were both already on their way back to sleep.

They took their time over breakfast. Even when Tom was busy his workday started late, a minor benefit in the life of a young attorney. That morning Sophie scrambled eggs and served them on whole wheat toast. So far as she could discern, their silence at the table was a comfortable one.

In the first days after she'd gone to get his father from the hospital, Tom had withdrawn from Sophie. She'd taken him then to be angry, which made sense to her, though she still believed she had done the only thing she could. After another day of his detachment she suspected that he felt more embarrassed than anything else. She had seen something that he had meant to keep hidden forever from her. She wanted to say, *He can't show me anything that will make me love you less.* She wanted to say, *Nothing needs to be hidden between us.* But she only said, "He's dying. He won't be around much longer."

Tom had not responded one way or another to the news. Nor had he asked about her time with Crane, what they'd talked about, what his own father was like. He didn't ask if they'd spoken about him. She had difficulty believing he didn't want to know these things. And yet he'd always insisted as much. Since the first days of their relationship, the topic had simply been off-limits. She didn't even know what terrible thing Crane had done to place himself beyond concern.

"I don't want you to see him again," he'd said. This wasn't precisely a command. Tom would never try to dictate her behavior, but he understood the force his wants held, a greater force than any command. And she didn't really wish to see Bill Crane again. There was something fearsome in it.

A week had passed before Tom was back to himself.

"Maybe I can come by the office this afternoon?" she asked now to break the silence. "For a cup of coffee or something?"

"I'd like that," he said, which she knew meant that it wouldn't happen. "Today's tough for me. We've got to take the summers to lunch, and those things go on forever, so I'll be tied to my desk when I get back."

Summers were the law school students who worked for the firm during their vacation. Tom had been a summer himself not so long before, and such terms of art were most of what Sophie knew about his job even now.

"Another time," she said. It was important that he know she didn't resent his unavailability, for it was part of the life they'd chosen, and after all she was often unavailable herself, in her own way. "I'll call."

They walked together as far as the subway stairs on Lexington, where Sophie left Tom before continuing another block to St. Agnes, the church she attended each morning. When she arrived for ten o'clock mass, five other congregants were scattered over the first three pews. There were the two widows, well into their eighties, who came to this mass every morning and always interceded during the prayer of the faithful on behalf of their husbands' souls. There was the middle-aged woman who came not every day but most with her son, who looked to be in his thirties, neatly dressed and cleanly shaven but distracted and childlike, his jaw circling beneath his face with compulsive stubbornness, indicating some vague disability.

Only the man in the second row wasn't a regular. Dressed in a suit and tie, his gray hair neatly slicked back, he knelt uncomfortably with his head bowed and his eyes pressed shut. His appearance suggested that he lived in the neighborhood, while his unfamiliarity to Sophie and the awkwardness with which he filled his pew suggested that he had entered the church impulsively that morning. Such figures weren't uncommon at St. Agnes, though their attendance was always short-lived. Sophie inevitably wondered what spiritual emergency—illness or death or some irrevocable act the guilt of which one wished to expiate—brought these supplicants to enact unfamiliar or long-abandoned rituals among strangers. But she put him out of mind and bowed her own head until the priest stepped out from the sacristy to begin mass.

Father Seneviratne was a shy, thoughtful man whose sometimes incomprehensible voice cracked while he sang the Gloria and the Agnus Dei. He'd come to the parish three years earlier, seeming serenely baffled that his vocation had led him thousands of miles from home to provide provisional comforts to wealthy whites on the Upper East Side of Manhattan.

A few weeks after his arrival, Sophie invited Seneviratne—Sameera was his first name, and he asked her to call him Sam—to the apartment for tea. As a convert she'd had little firsthand contact with the cultural trappings of the church. What she knew, or thought she knew, came from books, most of them more than a generation old. She had made the invitation assuming it was a custom when a new priest came to the parish, but Sam made it known while accepting that he had not received many other offers.

Two days later she waited outside the church after mass while he changed. He emerged from the parish house next door having traded his vestments and his collar for khaki pants, a button-down oxford shirt, and a blue blazer. He looked almost like a schoolboy, though Sophie guessed he was in his midthirties. He thanked her again for the invitation as they walked to the corner, passing what had once been tenement houses and were now single-family dwellings that routinely sold for millions of dollars.

"I'm glad to be here," Sam said, in response to a question that Sophie had not asked.

"It's a nice neighborhood," Sophie answered. She understood that he was speaking about an area broader than a few square blocks.

"You have lived here long? Since childhood?"

"Just since getting out of school a few years ago."

As they headed east, the townhouses gave way first to Park Avenue's apartment buildings, then the commercial stretches of Lexington and Third, and finally to the enormous high-rise on Second Avenue where Sophie lived with Tom.

"Are you from India?" she asked him as they rode the elevator upstairs.

"Sri Lanka," Sam said, and merely saying the words seemed to unlock something in him. By the time they were settled in the apartment, Sophie knew much of his life story. He had grown up Catholic—"My country has every type of religion," he said—and studied at a Catholic school in Colombo. He had decided to become a priest at a very young age. There had been a long civil war throughout his childhood, in which several family members had died, and the priesthood seemed the best way to escape to Europe or America. He said this without apology, without any sense that it was an imperfect reason for declaring a vocation. And why not? Sophie thought. He did work in the parish that no one else seemed inclined to do.

"For three years, I was in Ireland," he said, still marveling a bit at the very idea. "Now I am in New York."

And that was it. Sophie's turn had come, but she couldn't think of anything to say. Her privileged childhood in Connecticut horse country suddenly embarrassed her. Even the difficulties she'd faced seemed relatively meager. She considered saying something about her conversion, about her religious feelings, but it seemed overly intimate and anyway beside the point. Sam himself had spoken of the Church as an institution, of the things it provided his family and himself, but had not mentioned God.

So they sat quietly together, drinking tea and eating cookies that Sophie had bought for the occasion. It felt something like a first date, or what she imagined a first date would feel like, having never really been on one. She caught him staring over her shoulder, at the mess on her desk. She'd cleaned much of the apartment before his arrival, but left the piles of papers—her manuscript struggling to be born—as it was.

"I'm a writer," she said then.

"Really?" he asked. "You write? I am looking for a writer."

His whole body rose with excitement over the idea, and he started to speak more quickly, so that she struggled to understand him. He was raising money for a charity in Sri Lanka that found homes for children displaced by the war. There was a foundation that might help, but there was an application to be written, forms to be filled out, and his own writing wasn't strong.

"To be a writer is a very useful thing," he said. "If you are a writer, perhaps you can help?"

Three years later, Father Seneviratne—she thought of him this way only during mass; at all other times he was Sam—arrived at the altar, turned to the congregation, and greeted them.

It had taken time after Sophie's conversion for her to understand that many of the formalities she'd read about the Church belonged to a different era and were no longer practiced. Even then, she'd been surprised at how casual these weekday services could sometimes be. On some days she would have liked the priest to turn his back to her and intone in a dead tongue, the better to summon the necessary grandeur. But she had come to find in these short morning ceremonies something more practical in place of the sublime, just as she had come to see the holiness in Father Seneviratne, even though he admitted that his path to the priesthood had been directed by earthly concerns.

The mass was short, and on the way out Sophie shook Sam's hand and kissed him on the cheek before heading home. Back in the apartment, she sat at her desk and opened a notebook. She usually spent much of her day on the computer, doing research online, but she still wrote everything out longhand. It was the only way she could work. She was supposed to be finishing a draft of a proposal for a speech clinic that Sam had referred to her. The clinic worked with children with cochlear implants, born deaf and suddenly made to hear. In some cases, apparently, the complications that came with this gift were more dangerous than the disability itself. But Sophie's mind had wandered over the past week, and she'd written something very different.

The moment the phone rang she reached for it. Only then did she realize that she had been waiting all week to hear the sound, waiting for Bill Crane to call again.

"You're a hard girl to reach, Sophie Wilder."

Only one person called that number and used Sophie's maiden name.

"Greg," she said. "I haven't been avoiding you, I swear."

"Listen," he said, brightly. His manner was always

sweetness and light when he spoke to her. "I've been thinking about the follow-up."

"No kidding."

Most literary agents, as Sophie understood them at least, would simply forget about a writer who wasn't interested in writing. But her story collection had done very well by Greg, and he affected great loyalty to her. He might have better expressed that loyalty through tactful silence, she sometimes thought. The truth was that he hadn't done much to build on the success she represented for his own career, and he needed a follow-up, too. He had made a great show of understanding when she announced that she was abandoning years of work. But he was ready now for something to come of it. He called every few months to see how things were coming along, and he often had ideas for her.

"Have you thought of writing anything a bit more . . . autobiographical?"

She was certain they'd covered this before.

"You mean, a book about a twentysomething in New York, trying to write a book? That hasn't been done already?"

"People like stuff that's been done already. They know what they're getting. Besides, yours would have the female perspective. There's some novelty to that."

"Every time I base a character on myself, I kill her off halfway through."

What was clearly meant as a laugh came to her through the phone as an unhealthy wheeze.

"Kill her off, then. It will add some pathos."

"I'll think about it," Sophie said.

"The reason I bring this all up is that I had lunch with an editor a while back who gave me a new book that was getting a lot of buzz. I've just finished it, and it made me think of you. I mean, it isn't half as good as what you're capable of, but it's in a line that might work for you. I'll send it over, and you can tell me what you think."

"As a matter of fact," Sophie told him, "you don't need to bother. I've started on something, and it's coming along really well."

"That's great. Tell me about it."

Only when Greg showed genuine interest did his usual enthusiasm sound fake by comparison.

"To begin with, it's not autobiographical. It's about an old man. A lonely, dying old man, in a room by himself, haunted by mistakes."

"Sounds like a page-turner."

"I should probably get back to it, actually."

"Okay," Greg said. "Well, listen, I'll still send this book over just the same. It never hurts to scope out the competition."

He sounded uncertain of whether she was putting him on. Sophie wasn't sure herself. Where had she gotten the idea to say such a thing? She had spent much of the past week writing about Crane, but compulsively, with no intention of showing the results to anyone.

Once off the phone, she went over those pages, which she'd avoided doing before. The writing was clumsy, rough-draft writing. It was the first thing of this sort she'd written in a long time, and her tools had gone rusty and dull. The urge was strong to clean things up, to edit and arrange, but this would commit her to the idea of it, besides which there was little point, since none of it could go anywhere. It would be too cruel to Tom. She wouldn't have written anything if she'd allowed for the possibility of its being read by someone else.

It had only been a joke to get Greg off the phone. She wouldn't need to show those pages to him or anyone else.

But the mere idea of it stopped her short, and she knew she wouldn't get writing of any kind done that day.

The subway platform was mostly empty as the day neared noon, and she stood perfectly still, feeling the thick, warm underground air against her face. Then she heard the rattle in the distance and leaned out over the track to watch the two periods of light approach.

She had a book in her bag, and if she'd been headed anywhere—to run errands or to meet a friend for lunch—she would have taken it out to pass the time after entering the train and finding a seat. But she was riding now just to ride. She kept her bag closed between her legs and her attention on the car.

The subway, Sophie believed, was one of the few places on earth where one could observe the full array of humanity. All but the very wealthiest New Yorkers found themselves there from time to time. Even this late in the morning there were two men in expensive suits, reading the *Journal* on their way to work. There was also, at the opposite end of the train, a homeless woman, wrapped in a blanket despite the heat. Her hair was thickly matted, and the smell she gave off filled the car. She had entered at Grand Central, taken a seat, and started to sing to herself. The few people sitting nearby moved quickly away. Sophie wasn't near the woman, but if she had been she was sure she would have moved, too. To such people, she chided herself, the kingdom of heaven belonged. And yet it did no one any good—least of all the oblivious woman herself—to sit beside her, smelling the urine that soaked her socks, as though bearing witness. She kept singing until she got off at Astor Place, where the people near Sophie exchanged knowing and relieved looks.

By Spring Street most of the riders didn't know that the woman had been there a few stops earlier; they only knew that the car carried an unusually unpleasant smell. By Canal, even the smell was gone. This was another thing Sophie liked about riding: watching the different lives a train led over the course of its line.

"This is the last stop on this train," came the automated conductor's voice when they reached Brooklyn Bridge. "Everyone please get off the train."

Sophie stayed where she was as the rest of the car emptied out.

It had been years since she'd taken the six train to the end of the line, but there had been months, during the worst of it, when she did it almost every day. She would pass the subway stop on her way back from mass, and the prospect of going back to the apartment, back to work, was so daunting that she couldn't keep herself from going down the stairs, as if this train could take her anywhere.

This was all in her first years out of college, when she lived in a smaller apartment in the same building and Tom was uptown in law school housing. She was writing a novel then, because she had promised that she would.

"They're going to want rights to the big book, too," Greg had told her, as he prepared to send her story collection to publishers. Of course there would be a big book. Why wouldn't there be, since she was so young? She assumed as much herself.

The collection sold quickly to a publisher, with much competition. The author was herself a good story, orphaned and very young. The editor who won the bidding war wanted to play up the "wildness" the stories suggested.

It had been his idea to make the title story "Visiting Professor," with its intimations of lurid autobiography. Even her religious turn had its interest, a publicist had told her. ("It's like Graham Greene or something. I mean, who converts anymore? Unless they're converting *away*.")

Sophie refused to speak of it. Not out of shyness or embarrassment; she just didn't want to use her faith to sell a book. So the book sold without it. To Sophie, who half believed the whole world read the way she did, the numbers didn't sound very impressive, but everyone insisted they were. There were profiles and interviews and photo sessions. Awkward boys declared their loyalty on Web sites. All of this took up a year of her life, during which she did no writing at all, was not expected to, and so was free to imagine that it would all work itself out.

Around the time the stories came out in paperback, people began talking about the follow-up. Sophie had hundreds of pages of stories that hadn't been included in the collection, and they seemed similar enough in setting and style and tone to turn into something unified and whole. But when she sat down to the work in her second year out of school, it required that she imagine herself back into the girl who had written those stories, the girl who wrote in that voice they all liked so much. And this was beyond her powers. It should have been a simple matter of stitching, but the effort was excruciating. She couldn't believe that such work had once come easily.

Time passed around her. In Tom's last year of law school, they married and moved into a bigger apartment in her building. He went off each day, first to school and after that year to work, and her own days passed as they had before. Somehow, she spent two years—not decades, admittedly; not even an unusual gestation for a novel, but a good chunk of her life to that point—on a book that she'd known was dead before she'd started it. In truth, she had spent those years *with* the book, but not really *on* it. She still didn't know what she had spent the time on. She wasn't at all sure how it had happened.

The only thing that marked the days was the liturgy, which passed in and out of ordinary time, through Lent and Easter and Advent and Christmas. It was perhaps for this reason that she became a daily communicant during this period, though she had been rather casual about going to mass in the first years after her conversion. Back then, with the memory of the great transformation still alive within her, the terrestrial obligations of the faith seemed less pressing. But spending each day going over the things she'd written as a lost girl made her feel lost again, and so she started attending St. Agnes each morning, to remind herself of the force of her faith.

And then it was done. Two years of work had turned three hundred pages of good stories into two hundred and fifty pages of a terrible novel. When she announced that she was starting over, she expected anger or disappointment. She was ready to give all the money back. But her editor had since left the publishing house, so there was no one there to ask for it. She expected Greg, at least, to take her to task for all the time she'd wasted. Instead he confirmed his faith in her. She felt obliged to explain that whatever she did next wouldn't be much like the stories everyone had loved, because the girl who had written those stories didn't exist anymore. She had been regenerated. *Gennathei anothen* was the term, which she took to be not "born again," exactly, but "born from above." The follow-up, when it came, would likewise be born from a different place. This would be fine, he assured her. Even with a different point of view, a different set of values, she still had her *style*.

Which confused Sophie, although she didn't say as much. What was style, if not a point of view? A set of values? She'd been reading Augustine, who said that beauty consisted in fairness and fitness—the elegance with which a thing suited its proper ends. She understood this to mean that beauty itself could not be a proper end. Where did that leave style? How could she exchange every part of herself but that one?

This concern turned out to be academic, because she simply couldn't write, in any style. Sometimes an idea would be there in front of her, beautiful in its promise. But as she tried to transmit it, a kind of aphasia took her in its grip. The simplest objects and ideas turned ineffable. She couldn't name a character, describe someone as "tall" or "short," let alone participate in the alchemy by which such descriptions accrue into something like life.

Of all lies that she could have chosen to live, the lie that she was writing a book might have been the easiest to get away with. Out of superstition or for more practical reasons, most writers avoided discussing their works in progress, so people rarely questioned her. When they did, she sometimes said it was going well; at others she threw her hands up in frustration. But she was never pressed for specifics, by Tom or Greg or anyone else. No one even asked when she thought it would be done.

It was at this point that she had started riding trains. The hum of them quieted her distress. She mostly rode the local, but sometimes she transferred to the four or the five and continued on into Brooklyn. She might get off at Borough Hall and walk back into Manhattan over the bridge. On nice days the bridge would be crowded with tourists, stopping to take photos of each other while the cyclists threatened to run them down. She preferred the dark days, when she had long swathes of the walkway to herself. She would gaze out at the fog sitting low upon the river, wondering at the numinous beauty of it and remembering a time when the curtain had been ripped and she had briefly glimpsed the world beneath the world. She imagined a life composed entirely of riding and walking. She thought she could live such a life.

Then Sam had come to the parish, and to tea, to ask her to write on behalf of the charity in Sri Lanka. As it turned out, he had only wanted her to look over something he'd written, to fix it up, correcting his grammar and spelling. But once she got started she knew she would have to work from scratch. She bought books about grant proposals and spent time teaching herself the form. She researched other foundations that might be interested beside the small one that Sam had already found. Then she spent three weeks writing. In the end, $30,000 was sent to Sri Lanka. Something she'd written had made a difference in the world. Lives had been changed by words she'd set down. She asked Sam if he knew anyone else who needed her help, and she had a new job.

When she spoke of taking on freelance work—just something to fill the days when the novel wasn't coming along—Tom was encouraging. He'd been proud of her book's success but on balance mystified by her writing. He mostly knew that it wasn't going well. It wasn't important to him that she finish her book, only that she be happy. Anyway, she wasn't giving up on fiction; she was just taking some time from it. But the satisfaction of this new kind of writing, which seemed to represent her faith in action, was too great to set aside.

There was no grand pronouncement. She said nothing to the people who were waiting for the novel. But she gradually came to understand that she was done. She knew that she would easily enough be forgotten. Some of her stories might be anthologized somewhere, but the collection would go out of print and when it did Sophie Wilder would leave the shelves. Even Greg would forget eventually. He would find new clients or not, but either way he would give up on her. This was all a relief. In the meantime, she handled his quarterly calls, told him things were getting on track, and continued sending proposals to the grandchildren of robber barons, asking them to direct their families' money to parish soup kitchens or adoption programs. She had thought she was happy with the choice, which anyway hadn't felt like a choice, exactly. But all it had taken was one conversation to send her back to the trains, into the secret station.

The downtown six, after emptying out its last passengers at Brooklyn Bridge, continued on to the City Hall station, no longer open but still there, beautiful in its shining tiles. Sophie remembered the first time she'd discovered the place, an occult destination, it had seemed to her, another reminder of the world beneath the world. It always surprised her a little each time to find it still there. She sat alone while the train made its way through the station and back out at the Brooklyn Bridge stop on the uptown track.

Sophie rode from there with every intention of going back home, but when they reached Bleecker, she left the train and went upstairs. She knew before she was out on the street where she meant to go. When she reached Bill Crane's building, she rang the bell, and he buzzed her inside without asking who was there.

Halfway between the second and third floors, she got her first hints of the scent of pot in the stairwell, still familiar though it had been years since she'd smoked it and months at least since she'd so much as smelled it at a party. It had been present enough in her earlier life to summon now large blocks of the past. She thought of those days and imagined some young hipster couple living somewhere in the building among the Asian and Hispanic immigrants.

After a single knock and a brief rustling beyond, the door opened. Crane stood for a moment blocking the way, considering her. Even before the smoke followed after him, she knew from his face, the tired looseness about the jowls, that the smell had been coming from his apartment. His look of confusion slowly gave way to recognition, but he still didn't step aside to let her in. He couldn't have been expecting her back, but he didn't seem surprised to see her. He was simply fumbling over the meaning of her appearance.

"Come in, come in," he said after another moment, retreating into the apartment.

Her cleaning work had been entirely undone, the folders that she'd piled up were spread again across the floor, as if he'd been working with them. On the wooden coffee table, beside a pile of books, sat a glass ashtray that held a newly lit joint. He picked it up and took a pull as she closed the door behind her.

"Do you think that's a good idea?"

"Girlie, I'm dying," he said. "This is doctor-prescribed."

"Is that how it works now?"

She had been tempted to drink only once or twice in the years since giving it up, and not once to take drugs. But when he offered the joint in his hand she accepted without a thought, as though obeying the rules of his house.

"Have a seat," he said, clearing some books from beside him on the couch. And she did.

She took just a slow, shallow drag, wanting the taste in her throat but not to distance herself overmuch from the world.

"Does Thomas know you're here?"

He could have guessed the answer; he seemed to want her to admit it.

"No," she said. "And he wouldn't be happy if he did."

He took the joint from her.

"Tell me about him."

She couldn't begin to answer such a question.

"I suppose that if he wanted you to know, he would have come here himself."

He took this better than she might have expected.

"Tell me about yourself, then."

She had come uninvited and could hardly complain, but she didn't like this interrogation.

"I'm a writer."

"Oh, I know that," Crane said. "You're famous. Wrote a book about fucking older men."

She couldn't tell how maliciously he intended the look he now gave her. She handed the joint back to him.

"And what about your family?" he asked.

"What about them?"

He laughed. "Most of what you need to know of a person you can learn just by seeing how her folks turned out."

"They died years ago." She wasn't sure how much more to say. "It's just me and Tom. And Aunt Beth."

"Beth." He said the name as though it made her present in the room. "A fine woman, from what I remember. Always found her cold, though. And a bit of a religious nut."

"She's my godmother."

"Oh, yes. You're a convert? Do I have that right?"

Convert. From the Latin, to turn. As in Eliot: *Because I do not hope to turn again.*

She nodded, wondering uncomfortably where his knowledge of her ended.

"Was that Beth's requirement, or Tom's?"

"Neither." She didn't feel defensive; she only wanted him to understand. She took another drag before going on. "I didn't convert to marry Tom or anything like that. I chose to do it."

"But for Thomas's sake?"

"It hardly matters to Tom," she said. "I did it for myself."

She could see him struggling to make sense of it.

"I suppose it's some consolation?"

"Most of the time it scares the shit out of me."

This answer pleased him. The already deep wrinkles in his face deepened further as he smiled. She took the joint back and settled into the couch.

"It's funny," he said. "After all this time, people still can't do without God. I never would have guessed that He'd survive to your generation. Even the atheists are militant. They can't quite get over Him."

"Most of my friends don't think one way or another about it," Sophie told him. "They're not for it or against it; they're just beyond it."

"Two things fill the mind with ever new and increasing wonder and awe. The starry heavens above me and the moral law within me."

"You've got a real way with words," she said.

They had finished the joint, and she stubbed it out. It made a brief hiss where the ashtray was wet, and then it was done.

"That's Kant," he said. When she didn't respond, he asked, "How much do you know about me?"

She wondered what answer he would prefer. Perhaps he liked to be a mystery, liked surprising her with his own knowledge of her career while she had no commensurate knowledge about his.

"Only that you exist," she said. "And even that I'm a little fuzzy on."

How strange it really was, after all, that Tom should have said so little about his father. Though she wasn't sure how much Tom knew himself, since he wouldn't even admit to the extent of his ignorance. Her true betrayal might have been learning facts about Bill that Tom didn't know. And yet, what beside the desire to do so had brought her there?

"The *via negativa*," Crane said. "That's one way of approaching me."

If he meant to provoke her with this low-grade blasphemy, he would only be disappointed. After a long silence, he spoke.

"Do you believe in God? Or is it just the smell of incense that appeals to you?"

"No," she said. "I believe. And you?"

"Oh, I would have to believe in Him, to hate Him as much as I do."

She wasn't sure she had it in her then to do the excavation he seemed to be demanding. There was so much there—an entire life. All she knew of it now was that it would soon be done. She couldn't say how long the next silence lasted. And then she might have spoken, though she couldn't have said this for certain either. She had once enjoyed the sense of disconnection, the uncertainty about what had been communicated and what remained within, that came with getting high. Now it terrified her. She turned to find him carefully rolling another joint. He looked very old as he did it.

"What was that?" he asked.

"I'm afraid I need to go," she said. "I'm not sure why I came."

"Neither am I," he said before setting the makings of the joint on the table and walking her to the door.

She wanted him to ask her to come back, but she knew that he would not.

"Are you all right here alone?" she asked.

He seemed tempted to take offense, but instead he smiled. "It's a little late to start worrying about me."

She'd worried about him before she knew he existed. She would have said as much, but he was already closing the door. As Sophie walked down the stairs, she caught herself composing the scene in her head.

5

AFTER JUNIOR YEAR, Sophie rented an apartment in the Village with money left by her parents. She interned at a poetry press, and someone there introduced her to Greg, who would become her literary agent. I never met him, but he sounded like another of those young and prematurely jaded guys, just out of school, seemingly everywhere then, whose ranks I didn't yet know I would be joining. He was still an assistant, but he asked to read Sophie's stories and started sending them out. He sold one to the *Paris Review* and another to the *New Yorker*, guaranteeing Sophie a book contract. Her collection would allow him to give up answering the phone for his boss and take on clients full-time.

That summer I began a novel that would swell to a thousand pages before I abandoned it. Now graduated, Max started opening mail and answering phones for the weekly where he still works. He lived with three other guys in a loft on Thompson Street, a big, open space, nearly as suitable as Gerhard's house for crowded parties, which

Max and his roommates threw often. I want to say that this was the summer when all three of us came to see writing as a job rather than just as our way of being in the world. I want to say that we lost our innocence, and that afterward we weren't quite sure what the loss had bought us in return. That Sophie and I both realized, without admitting as much to each other, that the hermetic world in which we'd enclosed ourselves had begun to chafe. But it was all much simpler than that. This was the summer when Sophie fucked Max.

It happened in late August, a few weeks before we were due back at school. I'd been sick for a few days, and when I got better I went downtown to meet Sophie for lunch.

"How's the shut-in?" she asked.

"I'm feeling better," I told her. "Still mostly shut in."

She talked about her job, which she treated with amused detachment, offering character sketches of all the important people she was supposed to be trying to impress. But I could see she was uncomfortable about something. Outside the restaurant she said, "I've got some time still."

We walked a few blocks just north of Houston Street. With the university still out for the summer, and the dog days upon us, MacDougal was abandoned, its smoke shops empty except for the exotic water pipes in the windows, all looking alive and sinister.

"I stayed with Blakeman last night," Sophie said.

"What do you mean?"

"Max," she said. "I mean Max. I mean that I slept with him."

Her bluntness I recognize now as a kind of defense. She hoped the shifting nature of our relationship could protect her in the face of a bad mistake.

"You might have picked anyone else."

"It wasn't like that," she said. "It was late, and we were the last two left at the party. It wasn't a big thing."

She offered no apology. She didn't even allow that I might have expected one. Having followed her lead, I had no choice but to play along. Somehow I kept up conversation until we got to her office on Broadway. Then I went home.

A few days later, Max came to the apartment while my mother was out at work. At first he spoke vaguely about how Sophie and I weren't really together. He reminded me that I had told him about Sophie's interludes with other guys. I had even told him that they didn't bother me. But finally he recognized the thing for what it was, and he told me he was sorry. In the end, Max was Max. One couldn't expect all that much of him. We both knew that I would forgive him eventually. I didn't see either of them for the rest of that summer, and I don't know how much they saw of each other.

Back on campus for senior year, Sophie knocked on my door. When I answered, she started crying—something I'd never seen her do. I'd been waiting for her to come to me, to beg for my forgiveness.

"What is it?" I asked.

"I need your help."

"I'm sorry," I said. "I can't."

"It's not about Max," she said. "It's something else." Then she corrected herself. "I mean, it's not really about him."

"I don't care what it's about," I said.

"I'm pregnant."

The news took a moment to settle. It was plausible enough, but I wanted to think it was just another story, a rather conventional one, about the scared young girl who has gotten herself into trouble.

"Jesus Christ," I said. "Were you two really that careless?"

"Yes," she said. "We really were."

I think now of what might have been different in that moment. Even if I'd realized that this was my last chance with Sophie, I can't be sure I would have taken it. Maybe I was ready to throw off the life that we'd had, which now seemed insupportable to me. And perhaps I was right to feel insulted that she should expect me to help her bear up to the consequences of what she'd done with Max.

"I can't help you anymore," I said.

She looked startled in a profound way, as though the outcome of our conversation had never been in doubt to her, and a great many things now had to be recalibrated to assimilate this unforeseen turn.

"So we're not going to get over this?" she asked.

I didn't answer.

"Well what am I supposed to do, then?"

"What do you mean?"

"I made you," she whispered.

She was right, even if it didn't change anything to say it now. I asked her to repeat herself not because I thought I'd misheard but because I wanted to hear it again, wanted to take proper hold of the idea.

"I need you," she said.

We ran into each other on campus, but we didn't speak much until I went to Sophie's room in early winter. It was the beginning of December, almost exactly three years since Max's visit to campus. Over the years, her single rooms had been almost indistinguishable, but this one was different from the others, mostly just cleaner. There weren't papers and books all over the furniture and floor. There were no burning joints or cigarettes, no half-empty bottles.

"It looks nice," I said.

"Well, I can't do as much damage by myself."

"I guess not."

"Listen, Charlie. I'm so sorry."

"You don't have to," I told her.

"No, really," she said. "I'm sorry for all of it. I knew what I was doing. I'm sorry for pretending it didn't matter. And I'm sorry for coming to you to clean up the mess."

"About that part," I said. "I'm sorry, too."

She nodded, and that was all we said about it. I never asked what she'd done about the pregnancy.

"I thought you might like to stay with us for Christmas," I said. "It's become something of a tradition by now. And maybe we can work some things out, get ourselves back on track."

The invitation seemed to surprise her.

"I appreciate it, Charlie. But I have plans."

"You have plans?"

"I'm spending the break at Tom O'Brien's place," she said. "With Tom and his aunt."

Like that, she floated back out of reach.

In a certain way, I was glad that she'd chosen Tom, of all people. I'd been in a few classes with him, known him a little over the years. He was a quiet kid. Unimaginative, he seemed to me. He would not have impressed me even as one of her two-week indulgences from earlier years, and I doubted that he would last long.

"You guys are serious?"

"We've been together since fall break."

People had been keeping it from me, which suggested that my struggles over Sophie had been more apparent than I'd thought.

"You'd like him if you got to know him."

I doubted it.

"Sure I would," I said. "I've always followed you in matters of taste."

It took time to understand that Sophie wouldn't pass so quickly out of the Tom phase. I spent the rest of senior year trying to figure out what kind of person I was going to become, now that she wasn't watching. I dated a girl in the class below ours, one who still keeps in touch and who deserved better than the person I was that year.

One day I ran into my old roommate, Dean, who told me his parents had visited that weekend. They'd all gone to mass together, not at the campus chapel but at the church in town.

"I saw Sophie Wilder there, sitting in the back by herself. I didn't know she was Catholic."

"She's not," I said. "It must have been someone else."

"I know what she looks like," Dean said. "The two of you were inseparable when we lived together. It was Sophie."

I considered the possibility.

"It's probably for some story she's writing."

Later I would hear from others that she was going to mass regularly, never with other students, always in town. Some said she had spoken with the local priest about getting baptized, but this sounded like a rumor and I didn't think much about it.

After we graduated, Sophie published her story collection, which she dedicated to the memory of her parents. My name came right after Tom's on the acknowledgements page. The collection made her briefly famous, in the local, limited way that was all we could have wanted. The object of this fame was a girl I didn't really know anymore, but the occasion for it—those stories—I knew better than anyone, better perhaps than the author herself did. It was strange to watch it happen, to watch it pass, and to be left waiting just like any other fan for the big book to come out.

We sometimes wound up at parties together, but I didn't spend much time with our college friends, preferring the disaffected literary crowd that circled around Max. Amid that crowd Sophie's name came up occasionally. Some of them had met her the summer before and knew what had happened between us, but to others she was just the girl with the big book contract. They talked about her in the vaguely suspicious way we talked about young writers we hadn't read but whose reputations we'd decided were undeserved.

"We went to school together," I'd tell them. "We used to be good friends."

People remembered this, I guess, because as time passed they started to ask me, "What happened to Sophie Wilder?" And I'd just shrug, secretly asking myself the same thing.

It had all amounted to a little less than three years, and none of it needed to mean anything as time went by. But to me, it did. Those days with Sophie became a touchstone against which I measured the passing time, my relationships, my writing, and found it all wanting. This wasn't just nostalgia—though I might have idealized what we'd had, I didn't want to recover the past. It was the incompleteness of it that haunted me. The story wasn't finished.

I thought often of those words—*I made you*—that she might or might not have ever really said. Then I remembered the first weeks of freshman year, wandering through the bookstore looking for all the books she'd pushed on me. Sophie had been led in the same way by Lila the year before, and she'd come to campus hoping to meet someone with whom she could share these things. When that person failed to appear, she turned me into him. Perhaps this is why I felt that things had to have a different ending: she couldn't abandon her own creation.

If I'm falling into old habits here, becoming too precious or too literary, let me keep to the realm of hard fact. I can no longer imagine the person I was before I met Sophie, a boy whose father is still alive, whose mother is still fixed to the earth, not etherized and floating. My entire life before she caught up to me after class that day feels like backstory sketched in by Sophie while we walked through campus that afternoon. Sophie Wilder invented me.

As we walked Gerhard's dog down Mercer Street, I waited for Sophie to tell us back into ourselves. But the story she told was a different one. It was about Tom's father, a man named Bill Crane, and it began with a telephone call. Sophie recounted delivering Crane from the hospital, taking him to his apartment and helping him to bed. She spoke about cleaning up the kitchen and the papers on his floor. She described the foreboding she felt, witnessing his disheveled life.

This was fine, so far as it went. Her story didn't have to have anything to do with us. It was just the kind we might have told each other after passing some tired, middle-aged man on the street. I could have picked up the thread halfway through and somehow known how everything turned out between Bill Crane and his daughter-in-law. I was happy just to be walking with Sophie again. We headed east on Bleecker, back uptown on Broadway, then east again toward Tompkins Square. We moved with no logic that I could discern, neither one guiding the other, just as we always had. But some intention on her part, conscious or not, led us to an old tenement on the Lower East Side.

"This is it," Sophie said.

"What?" I asked.

"Crane's building."

I looked it over carefully, as though I already understood I would be called upon to give an account of the place. The front of the building was white up to the top edges of the first-floor windows, painted in broad, careless roller strokes, with workmen's hands still visible in the paint's lined unevenness. After the first floor the crumbling red brick was uncovered. On a few levels potted plants or flower boxes had been placed out on the fire escape, and there were colored plastic lights and a statuette of Mary in the ground-floor window nearest us.

Sophie didn't point out Crane's window, but I tried to imagine his apartment from what she'd told me. The conditions she'd described weren't much different from the ones in which we had once lived together, in which I lived still. Even if I didn't mean to be living that way in another thirty years, I wasn't eager to acknowledge the tragedy of such a life.

As we stood there, the curtains of the ground-floor window opened. An old woman's face appeared, surrounded by the lights and the statuette, seeming to flicker in and out of existence. It wasn't an unkind face, but there was something terrifying about it. Sophie grabbed my arm and led me away. The woman's appearance in the window seemed to deflate Sophie. Our walk was over then, and we took the shortest route back to Washington Square.

When we arrived, Max was smoking a joint on the couch and watching *The Third Man*. He paused the DVD and asked how our morning had been.

"We played *flâneur*," Sophie said. "It was exhausting. I'm entirely out of practice."

She headed for the stairs. I watched Max watching her go before I joined him on the couch. He turned the movie back on and offered me the nub of his joint, which I declined. On the screen, Joseph Cotten was calling toward a darkened doorway in bombed-out Vienna. A woman upstairs turned on a light to reveal Orson Welles's sly face, looking almost embarrassed by its own charm.

"Probably due for a reconsideration," I said.

Max looked quizzically at the joint that had gone out in his hand.

"It's a fine performance," he said, "but I always preferred him in those Mondavi wine commercials."

"I followed his shadow," Joseph Cotten explained. "Till suddenly, well, this is where he disappeared."

When *The Third Man* ended, Max started it from the beginning. He never went out to the movies except to see something he was assigned to review, but he could sit on this couch watching an old favorite three or four times running. He reached a kind of fugue state; people would enter and leave the house, and he would give no sign of noticing.

We were still watching when Sophie came down with a new outfit on—a sleeveless top and dark skirt that reached just below the knees. She looked rested but subdued. There was a slackness to her, as if she were waking up from a long sleep.

"You look beautiful," I said, which was true but beside the point. She gave an ironic curtsy to diffuse the embarrassment of my remark.

"We're grabbing something to eat," I told Max. "You're welcome to join us."

"That's all right," he said. "I've got to write a blog post about the cuckoo clock speech."

He would have easily forgotten his work if he'd wanted to join us, but I was glad that he'd let us go. Even after all the time that had passed, I couldn't sit at a table with the two of them; I wanted Sophie to myself. "Behave, kids," Max said as I got up. "Keep the Holy Spook between you."

We'd planned to get something nearby, at one of the Italian places on Sullivan or Thompson. But it was a beautiful, cool evening. Relief had finally come after a punishing summer only a few weeks gone, and we decided to walk. I told Sophie that I'd read the latest novel by our visiting professor from freshman year.

"Do you still speak with him?" I asked.

"He never even kissed me," Sophie said. "Even that part I made up." She laughed as though at a childhood eccentricity, but it seemed painful to her to remember. "I really didn't know the difference back then. I couldn't recognize the truth when I saw it."

"Sure you could," I said. "But you were a fiction writer."

"If that's what it means, then I'm glad I've given it up."

I couldn't tell by the way she spoke if she wanted to talk about it. "You're really done?" I asked. "Not just with this book?"

"With everything."

It made me desperately sad to hear this. We had been so certain once.

"It's not too late," I said, as much to myself as to her. "There's always hope."

"Endless hope," she answered. "But not for us."

On Clinton Street we passed a newly opened restaurant that had been written up in Max's magazine the week before. It was recommended as a place to take a first date you were trying to impress, but I didn't say this to Sophie when I suggested we try it. The hostess told us we'd have to wait for a table, so we found two seats at the bar. Sophie ordered us each a Jameson.

"Your Irish," I said.

"My Irish," Sophie said. "You must think I'm a terrible backslider."

"To be honest, I never understood why you quit. Most of the people we knew were worse off than we were."

"I made a few mistakes," she said. "They turned out to have some real consequences."

We sat in silence until our drinks came. Once they did she raised her glass to me.

"Anyway, I've done my penance. I can start making mistakes again."

I touched my glass to hers.

We didn't say much after that. I thought of long hours spent communing in quiet sadness. It would be easy to say we had just been two unhappy kids who'd both lost parents, seeking comfort in each other. Plenty of our classmates thought as much when they puzzled over our strangely intense relationship. But I missed the particular brand of unhappiness I had felt in those years.

We were into our second round by the time a table was ready for us.

"What are you writing these days?" Sophie asked. "How's your follow-up?"

"I tried to get started on something right away," I said. "But I spent too much time thinking about how everything was going to change when the book came out. Maybe I wanted to be another Sophie Wilder."

"She was something, wasn't she? What ever happened to her?"

"It didn't take long for the image to get swept away. But I can't really figure out what to do next. It doesn't seem to matter either way, since no one's reading my work."

"I did."

"But I didn't know that."

"It came at a complicated time," Sophie said. "But I should have been in touch, just to tell you congratulations."

I thought I knew what complications she was talking about. A few months after the book came out, a friend told me that Sophie and Tom had split up. I didn't know the circumstances, but I couldn't help imagining it had something to do with me, that Sophie too had used our days together as a touchstone and found her life wanting. It would be wrong to say that the idea pleased me, but the timing of the news gave me hope that the book's release might be the occasion for her return.

"It's not that I ever expected to become a celebrity," I said. "But I looked around at the people I knew, the few people left who were supposed to care about these things, and even they didn't give a shit. I just wanted to matter to someone in the way these things mattered to us."

I hadn't spoken about this before, hadn't even entirely known that I'd felt it. But Sophie would understand, even if no one else did. And yet, what help could she offer me, when she'd already given up on herself?

"You'll get it all straightened out," she said. Her tone was not encouraging or insistent. She spoke as though from the future, reporting a simple and certain fact that she expected to be treated as such.

After dinner, we wandered back to Gerhard's, where we found Max and a crowd of others, drinking and laughing in the living room.

"You do this every night?" Sophie said in mock disgust.

"We try to," Max said.

"Did you finish your post?" I asked him.

"It's a fucking blog."

"Granted," I told him. "But it's part of the conversation."

"Somehow the conversation goes on apace without me. My commenters are having it out about *The Pirates of the Caribbean* as we speak."

I didn't feel up for another evening of Max and our friends, but Sophie was already on her way to the kitchen for a drink. I waited for her on the couch, beside the aquarium.

The tank was nearly ten feet long and three feet tall, held up on legs of turquoise brass with Art Nouveau embellishments that called to mind the entrance to a Paris metro station. Mossy vegetation grew up from its floor. There was nothing in the way of playful accoutrements within, no sunken treasure or deep-sea explorers in diving bells. The world was designed for its inhabitants, not for the spectators above. I didn't know much about the half-dozen fish that occupied the tank, except that they were rare and that Gerhard had given careful instructions for attending to them. Properly speaking, this was Max's job—my job was the dog—but he often forgot, so I tried to keep an eye out. Occasionally a drunken guest tapped crudely against the glass, but even this drew little response from the fish, who went about their lives, oblivious to the giants all around them, under whose attention they swam.

Sophie returned with two glasses of whiskey.

"Aren't you going to introduce me to your crowd?" she asked.

I began with Morgan Bench, an old friend of Max's who had gained some local notoriety while working for a daily gossip column, crashing parties, and misbehaving.

He had since given up the job to write screenplays, but his reputation remained. He was thought of as irresistibly rakish, in the manner of a character in an old screwball comedy, and sometimes he was. But the persona didn't come entirely naturally to him. He was at heart a better person than he wanted to be. That night, Morgan was dressed for brunch at a New England yacht club: Nantucket reds, loafers without socks, a blue blazer with a white pocket square. But under the blazer he wore a tight pink T-shirt with a drawing of Miss Piggy on it.

"Morgan," I said, "this is Sophie O'Brien, an old friend of mine."

"You've heard about Sophie," Max said, correcting my inadequate introduction. It was important to Max, when curating crowds, that everyone be given a proper role. "She's a wonderful writer. Writes under her maiden name, Wilder. You remember that collection, *Visiting Professor*, that got all that attention a few years back?"

Morgan looked up at the ceiling and twitched his nose as though he had an itch he couldn't reach.

"Did they make a movie?"

"A few of the stories were optioned," Sophie said. "But nothing came of them. They wouldn't translate very well to the screen, to be honest."

Morgan looked her over sympathetically.

"Maybe next time," he said. "Anyway, you've got very nice tits."

"They wouldn't translate to the screen, either."

Max left me to talk with Morgan while he guided Sophie to Colleen Lawrence, a staff writer at his magazine. It seemed from Colleen's response that she was familiar with Sophie, perhaps had even read her work. Watching them talk, I imagined her asking what Sophie was working on now, while Sophie shrugged modestly, invoking the writer's sacred right to secrecy. I had the sense one sometimes gets when watching a television on mute of the fundamental absurdity of even the slightest human gestures. I remembered the feeling I used to have watching Sophie from a distance on campus, when it seemed a travesty for her to be out in the world, interacting like a normal human being. But she had somewhere acquired that necessary adult talent for holding the better part of herself in reserve while offering enough of a face to keep the world fooled. It seemed that I'd made a great mistake in thinking that I had special access to the part of Sophie that remained hidden from everyone else. I may have seen a layer that others didn't know, but the true depths remained forever unavailable.

Beside Colleen stood Marvin Alexander, a Web designer who also played drums for a passable alt-country band. After they had spoken for a few minutes, Max brought her around to the rest of the group, mostly people I knew only vaguely or not at all. It was never clear to me where Max found the people who filled out those nights, or whether he found them at all. Perhaps they just appeared as needed. But inevitably Max knew them, or made some show of knowing them. It was part of his job. Though we lived there together, he was always the host.

I exchanged a few crude jokes with Morgan, but when he went in search of a cigarette I retreated to the fish. I was watching them when Sophie approached in the reflection of the glass, walking unsteadily in the frame of the tank's brass borders. She'd refilled her drink.

"Now you've met the whole sick crew," I said.

"I have."

"And what do you think?"

"What do I think?" She looked at the tank as though the answer were there. She pointed at Morgan, making no effort to conceal the gesture. "I think that he's Sebastian Day."

This was the name of a minor character in my book, based entirely on Morgan.

"Guilty," I said.

"And the girl in black, Colleen, is Sarah Staple."

Colleen and I had dated around the time I was writing the novel, and she had found her way to a more prominent part in the book. This time I didn't even bother admitting to it.

"Marvin is Paul Tanner. Though you turned him into a bass player, which hardly seems fair. Drummers are so much sexier."

"What about him?" I asked, pointing to a tall, ungainly guy with a shaved head. He was standing next to Max with an odd smirk on his face, taking in the whole party much as we were. I had noticed him talking to Sophie earlier, but as far as I knew we had never met before.

Sophie didn't skip a beat.

"But that's a trick question. He's a character escaped from an entirely different book."

I wanted to say that she was wrong, that it wasn't as simple as all that. But it had been precisely that simple. I'd written exactly the kind of book that Sophie hated so much: real-life experience thrown down on the page without any transformation. I'd started it after giving up on the enormous, unwieldy thing I'd been working on since meeting her, the novel that had grown out of our hours of writing and talking together. By the time I abandoned that other work and started over, I was tired of invention. I'd exhausted my imagination. Some scenes in the new one were nearly word-by-word transcriptions of stoned conversations in Max's old loft or petty frustrations at the office where I'd temped while writing it. I don't know how Sophie could tell this, since she hadn't been following my life and had never met any of the people I'd written into the book. It must have been apparent just by reading it. She had confirmed all my worst fears about my writing.

All the worst things about Sophie—her capriciousness, her streak of cruelty, her unwillingness to let pass even the most venial aesthetic sins—came back to me. If it had been wrong not to let her be just another girl once in a while, perhaps it had been wrong of her to hold me to her own standard, when we both knew that she had a talent I didn't possess.

"At least I haven't stopped trying," I said.

When I looked over at her, she was staring into the tank, transfixed by the elegant, oblivious movements of the fish, or else by her own reflection. "I should head up," she said. "I'm not used to late nights anymore."

"I'm sorry," I said. "I'll come up, too."

"No, stay here. Have fun with your friends. There's always tomorrow."

So I did stay. I walked over to the tall man I'd seen Sophie talking to. I realized as I approached that I did know him after all. He was a member of Marvin's band. He'd always worn long hair before, and I hadn't recognized him with his shaved head. Everyone always knew everyone at these parties, in the end.

Once Sophie was gone, things seemed just as they always were on those nights. More people arrived, until the whole first floor was filled. I stayed up late, though I was tired, and tired of those nights. If someone had told me that there would soon be an end to them for me, I would have been relieved.

6

SOPHIE DECIDED TO wait for her head to clear before calling Tom at work. There came instead a thickening of her senses, followed by sleep. She was still asleep when the alarm sounded the next morning. She lay unmoving until Tom shook her lightly back into the world.

"How you feeling?" he asked.

"All right," she said.

"You look sick."

And sick she felt, but she knew the aching in her throat and chest would pass before morning did. Tom pressed a hand to her forehead and pursed his lips with a look of concern. Sophie was sure she had no fever. Tom left the room without a word. A few minutes later he returned, with tea and a plate of toast.

"You're very good to me."

She said this just to recognize his gesture. She didn't mean anything in particular by it.

"Do you think so?" Tom asked. "I worry sometimes."

"You worry?"

"That I'm not around enough. That it's not good for us."

"You're busy right now," she said. "I'm busy too."

If she told him then about going to see his father, the few words they'd spoken so far that morning might still disappear as though they'd never been. By waiting, she let their talk solidify into a deception. Not having mentioned it sooner would become another thing to answer for. Finished with her toast, Sophie stood and went to the shower.

Back in the room, Tom was dressed—not for work but in jeans and a polo shirt.

"I called the office," he said. "I told them I wouldn't be coming in until the afternoon."

"Are you sure?"

She still didn't entirely understand the rhythms of his job. He had worked late every night since the summer started, but he could make time easily enough when the situation demanded it.

"I've got a few things I can do from here, and everything else can wait."

"Really, I'm not feeling that bad," she said. "I think that shower did the trick."

"Even better. We have the whole morning to ourselves."

Tom assumed that her schedule could open in simple answer to his. Whatever work she had was her own work, and so it could wait for another time. She was annoyed by the assumption even when it was right, and in this case the timing really was bad. She'd written nothing for the speech clinic, nothing about the deaf made to hear and how proper funding might help them also to speak. But time was short only because it had been wasted on Bill Crane—thinking about him, writing about him, visiting him. To be suddenly jealous of her hours when Tom made claims on them would mean choosing the father over the son.

They headed west, passing the subway stairs and then St. Agnes, throwing off routine together. In Central Park they walked beneath a cathedral of elm boughs through which fell panes of summer sun. An older couple went hand in hand in front of them, and Sophie reached for Tom, feeling a kinship with these two. She had the sense that she'd seen a picture of Tom's future. Or rather, a negative image of it, for he was nothing like his father. She wanted to tell him about her visit just to tell him this: you are nothing like the man; you will never be anything like him.

At school, her friends had taken Tom O'Brien for another diversion. Perhaps he had taken himself for as much when he sat down with her in the empty dining hall. Only Sophie had known that her break with Charlie was different this time. She had tested the limit, had always been testing, leaving and returning. Finally she'd broken through, and the limit was marked. But the act was irrevocable. She couldn't remember after the fact why it had needed doing, but she had been sure when she'd done it. It was like a secret told in a dream that one struggles upon waking to recover.

By the time Tom invited her home for Christmas things were "serious" between them, as she told her friends, though she wasn't taking anything quite seriously since breaking with Charlie and losing the child. She felt separated from her own life, unreal to herself. But she remembered their earlier stay at Beth's as a brief stretch of contented attachment amid all this floating, and she was hopeful as they drove down, looking forward to the two empty weeks ahead. She hadn't written anything all semester, the longest spell in years, since before her parents died. But Greg was happy with the collection they'd started putting together, and this counted for something. Work was being done on the stories, even if she wasn't the one doing it. In the trunk was a bag of books. If she still couldn't write, she would spend those weeks reading.

On the first night, she lay down in bed with a novel, uncertain and tentative, as if taking up a new habit rather than doing something that had consumed her life to that point. She fought to give herself up to it, knowing that the very need to fight was a guarantee that the effort would be wasted. Each word came through clearly enough, but when she tried to relate it to the ones that came before and after, to make meaning out of this relationship, she couldn't sustain the thread. She chose another book and ran through the same process again. She was panicked now, which only made concentration harder. For the first time she worried that the change in her, the distance between herself and her own life, was permanent.

She turned to the shelves beside the bed and looked over the titles, going more carefully through them now than she had during her earlier visit. She had not read a single one of them. She chose Thomas Merton's *The Seven Storey Mountain* because the title was familiar to her. The book's story wasn't unlike hers in broad outline. Merton had lost both parents before becoming an adult, and he had followed that loss with years of wild behavior. A child had been conceived. But these parallels should not have been enough to keep her interest where everything else failed, especially since her own life interested her so little. What struck her instead were the odd asides, spoken from a different world. Early in the book, she read a line about the "pattern and prototype of all sin": "the deliberate and formal will to reject disinterested love for us for the purely arbitrary reason that we simply do not want it." This was exactly what she had done to Charlie with Max. It had not been an experiment or a game or even a mistake: it had been a rejection of love. She had sinned.

Sophie would come in time to know all the famous conversions that had arrived by way of books. *Tolle lege*, a voice urged Augustine. Take up and read. St. Ignatius lay in bed, recuperating after his leg was shattered in battle by a cannon ball. He asked for romance novels to pass the time, but instead he was given a life of Christ. Later, on the rare occasions when she was asked to give an account of what had happened to her, she told the story in this way, tracing it back to the moment she came upon Merton's book. It was easier this way; it fit into people's ideas about her, and their ideas about intellectual respectability, to say that she'd been convinced by an argument on the page.

The truth was more difficult to explain. She continued reading because she found the book interesting, nothing more. There had been no change within her yet. When she'd finished—it took her most of a day—she looked at the other titles on the shelf. Not all of them were religious, strictly speaking. There were novels from the thirties and forties by French writers whose names were vaguely familiar. There were works of history and social thought. But it took only a moment of skimming to know that they had all been written from a Catholic perspective. It occurred to Sophie that an entire strain of human feeling and thought had been up until then utterly foreign to her. In the absence of stronger inclinations, it seemed worth getting to know. So she picked another book.

That week she learned about the difference between natural and revealed religion, between the God who could be approached through logic and the God who must present himself to us. She learned about the founding of the Church with Peter at its head.

What little she'd known of Christianity before came by way of writers like Milton and Dante. But Dante was Christian in the way that Virgil was pagan; it was a historical peculiarity one worked through to arrive at their timeless poetry. She felt as if she were visiting the modern Mediterranean armed only with Ovid as a guide.

Sophie's parents had not been religious—they lacked the feeling for it, what she would learn to call the *capax Dei*, the capacity to experience God—and so she had not been in many churches. When she and Beth and Tom went to mass in town on Christmas morning, the only point of comparison she had was St. Agnes, where she had gone with the Blakemans the previous three years. Christmas mass was a great performance there, a concert with professional singers accompanied on an enormous pipe organ. The Blakemans took this family tradition seriously enough, but gave no sign of real belief.

The church that Beth attended was small, the music amateurish but heartfelt. Where the priests at St. Agnes had been professorial, this one was a kind of tradesman. If you took away his vestments, it would have been easy to imagine him on a construction site or the back of a fire truck. He seemed at once to command the ceremony and to be an awed participant in it.

It is in the nature of what happened next that it can't be conveyed in words. The few times Sophie tried to explain it later, even to herself, she fell back on cliché: something came over her; she walked out changed. It got closest to it to say that she was, for a time, occupied. After all her reading in the week leading up to that day, she thought of that occupying force as the Holy Spirit. But mostly she knew that it was something outside of herself, something real, not an idea or a conceit or a metaphor. Once it passed on, she knew that her very outline had been reshaped by it, that this reshaping had been long awaited though she hadn't recognized as much. More than that, she knew that she wanted the feeling back. She would chase it forever if need be. Everything later followed from that. That was the part she couldn't explain to others. It couldn't be explained. It didn't come from books; it didn't allow itself to be argued for or against. In the remaining week of their vacation, she didn't mention it, though she fully expected that people could tell just by looking at her.

She had never entirely regained the feeling she'd had that day, but she still believed with certainty that it was real. She had to believe it, because she had built her life around it, and she couldn't accept that this was just another stage, just another life she might have chosen after the last one fell away. So she waited for that feeling to return. In its absence, she had her daily rituals. She had the form of faith.

"What's on your mind?" Tom asked as they continued through the park.

Sophie wanted to say she was thinking of him. Why didn't she think of Tom when she thought of that time? It had all happened under his watch. Perhaps she didn't think of him because he was still there. What she remembered, she remembered for its absence.

"I was thinking of our first Christmas at Beth's."

He slowed a little in stride, as though she had placed an obstacle before them. "What made you think of that?"

Those days brought different associations for Tom. He would have in mind the conversation they'd had a few days after Christmas, while Sophie was still dizzy with light. He would have in mind the first and only time they spoke about his father.

Sophie had come upon Beth in the hall, looking at the photo of Tom on his mother's hip.

"She was beautiful," Sophie said. It wasn't just something to say. The woman in the photo *was* beautiful, in the same way Tom was beautiful.

"I miss her every day," Beth said.

"There was a fire?" Sophie asked.

It was strange to admit that she didn't know more than this. She should have by then, though they'd only been together for weeks. Beth seemed to think so as well. Sophie's ignorance suggested trouble to her, whether Tom's or Sophie's own.

"He was eight when the house burned down. That's when he came to live with me."

Sophie might have asked anything then, and Beth would have answered. But she knew she ought to bring her questions to Tom. She had waited for him to tell her more about his parents, but he'd said nothing. Neither of them spoke much about the past. He knew about Charlie, of course. She had told him about the pregnancy and the miscarriage, though she'd let him assume that Charlie was the father. He didn't ask questions about her parents. He didn't ask questions about anything, really. She liked this then, and she tried to repay in kind.

That night in his room she spoke at greater length about her parents' accident and what it had done to her than she ever had to anyone before. Tom tried to comfort her while she spoke, but she didn't need comforting. She needed him to know how it happened and to hear it from her.

"Tell me about the fire," Sophie said into his sweater while he held her against his chest. "Tell me about how your parents died."

"My mother."

"What's that?"

"Only my mother died in the fire. My father got out."

She didn't know what to say. She wasn't sure she'd been lied to, strictly speaking, but she had certainly been deceived. The fact that he could let her persist in such misunderstanding suggested something worrying.

"What happened to him?"

"He left me to live with Beth. I guess he wasn't up for it. We never saw him again."

"That was it? He just disappeared?"

"More or less."

"Is he still alive now?"

"So far as I know."

"Do you ever think of finding him?"

Sophie had never seen Tom angry before. Even now the moment passed quickly. But something important about him had shown itself.

"I don't want to talk about it."

"We don't have to talk about it now," Sophie said.

"I don't ever want to talk about it."

Until then, she had liked that she didn't need to con-textualize herself for him, didn't need to marshal the facts of conventional characterization, to expend the effort of making herself present from moment to moment. He already had his own idea of her, and he didn't notice how she sometimes flickered. But she had liked it only because it had suited this strange time in her life. She wasn't sure she wanted to commit herself to such a stance forever, and this is what he seemed to be proposing. Their lives, he seemed to say, had begun on the day he sat beside her in the dining hall. Nothing before then needed to matter. But her parents mattered to her, after all, even in their absence, and she wanted them to matter to him, even if he could never meet them. The past could not be banished at will, even if they both wished for it to be. She was helped along in accepting his offer by the fresh recollection of what had happened in that church. A new life had indeed begun.

Sophie had honored the arrangement all these years, in spirit and letter both. Not only had she not asked Tom anything, she had resisted the temptation to ask Beth about Bill Crane, or to search for him online. It was this practice of restraint that kept her from looking through the folders in Crane's apartment. But everything seemed to have changed now.

"Tell me about your father."

Tom let go of her hand but otherwise made no response.

"I'm your wife," Sophie said. "How could I not want to know?"

"Ask him yourself, then."

"If you don't want to tell me, okay. But don't blame me for caring about your life."

Appeals to Tom's decency and reason were almost unfair, since he was the most decent and reasonable person she knew. She was near to apologizing, telling him he didn't need to explain himself, when he spoke.

"What did he tell you?" he asked. "About the past, I mean. About me."

"Nothing," Sophie said.

"He didn't say anything about the fire?"

"No."

Tom paused for a moment, considering a proper angle of approach.

"They met in grad school in Missouri. My father was studying philosophy and my mother was studying literature. They were finishing their dissertations. He was invited to stay on as an assistant professor. My mother did postgrad work until I was born. They got a little house out in the country, a rental, where we would stay for a week or two at a time over breaks, so my parents could write. That's where the fire happened."

For a moment it seemed that was all he would say, though he'd only repeated the few facts she already knew. But he was working on the proper expression of something that had been inchoate within him for years.

"He did it."

Sophie wanted to say something to acknowledge the enormity of the thing she'd forced out of him, but there was nothing to say. She wrapped her arm around his unyielding body.

"Maybe it was an accident," Tom said, as if the distinction hardly mattered. "He was drunk and stoned at the time. He might have fallen asleep with a joint or something. There was a trial. Not for arson, for negligent homicide. He was sentenced to two years. That's when I came to live with Beth. I waited for him to get out, so that I could have my father back again. I was ten or eleven by then. I remember it well. But when he was released, he just disappeared. We never heard a thing."

"I'm so sorry, Tom. It must have been awful."

"After a while I got over it. I just stopped waiting. Beth gave me all the affection or attention or whatever that a kid needs. I didn't feel some great loss. It was just how I grew up."

As if this desperate invocation of a happy childhood had required an objective correlative, they came then to the great brass sculpture of Alice on a toadstool, lording over the Mad Hatter and the March Hare. It was one of their favorite places in the park, and Tom walked ahead now, not away from her so much as toward the statue. He wasn't trying to be difficult, Sophie thought. He didn't want the story to mean anything, and so he refused to give it shape. She kept her pace and didn't catch up to him until they were both at the sculpture. Tom sat slumped like a weary child on one of the toadstools, his posture seeming to say that this was not what he'd skipped work to do.

"I'm sure he felt guilty. I'm sure that time was hard for him. But I needed my father back. I needed him to be strong enough to come back. Instead he made me feel like both my parents had died. So that's the way I decided to treat it. If he's dying now, it has nothing to do with me."

Sophie sat down beside him and took his hand.

"I shouldn't have made you talk about it."

She wasn't sure how he would feel about having finally told the thing, or how she felt about hearing it. But he let her hand surround his, and he looked almost tenderly at her. He was finished with the topic now, and he led them out of the park.

Over lunch at a diner on Madison, Tom seemed unburdened. He told stories about his bumbling summer associates, and the topic reanimated him. This was the Tom that Sophie loved best, funny in his largehearted way, but it was strange to see how quickly he got over this thing he'd avoided talking about for years. He spoke now as though everything between them had been settled. She decided not to tell him about her trip downtown, treating the omission as a kindness rather than a deception.

At her desk that afternoon, after seeing Tom off to work, Sophie thought of Bill Crane. She was glad the story was out, but she wasn't sure what to make of it. Could the man she'd met really have set that fire on purpose? Had he killed his own wife? An accident seemed more likely. And an accident, even a negligent one, made Crane an entirely tragic figure in her eyes.

Sophie tried to imagine how he would have felt getting out of prison, struggling to start a new life. She thought she understood why he might undertake that struggle alone. Perhaps he knew that Tom was better off with Beth. Perhaps it was a kind of selflessness, however misguided, that kept him away all those years. Sophie remembered what Crane had told her, about hating God, and she imagined that she understood now the origins of this hatred. As she imagined all this, she started to write.

"Hello?"

"Sophie Crane?"

It was like something out of a dream, hearing her name mixed with his.

"Lucia," she said.

"Miss Crane," said Lucia Ortiz. "I'm calling about your father."

"Is everything all right?"

"He didn't come down from his apartment the last few days, so I went up to check on him, and he didn't answer the door. The landlord and I went in to look for him. He's very sick. Maybe he hasn't moved for a long time. The ambulance just came for him."

"Where are they taking him?"

"To St. Vincent's."

"I'm on my way now."

In the three weeks since Tom had told her the story, she had continued to think of Crane, and to write, but she hadn't been back to see him. She had promised herself she would go if he called, but she'd known that he wouldn't call. Now her behavior felt disgraceful. She had cared more for the story than for the man.

She found the doctor's card in her purse. She called with little hope of getting through, but the woman answered on the second ring.

"I'm sorry to hear all this," Dr. Phillips said in her professional voice after Sophie had explained everything.

"It's fine that you're sorry," Sophie answered, surprising herself with her anger. "But what are we supposed to do?"

"Your father-in-law is not my patient anymore." The woman spoke as if to a troublesome child. "I suppose he hasn't told you that. After I went over the results of the last surgery, I recommended the gastrectomy, but Mr. Crane refused. I suggested some alternative treatments, and he refused those as well."

"So that's it?"

"Well, I also recommended hospice care. If he's not interested in a more aggressive approach, this is the only alternative, especially since he has no family to care for him." She let this remark linger. "But he refused this, too. He said he wanted to be left to die at home."

"And you're going to let that happen?"

"He's a grown man. As far as I can tell he still has full mental capacity. If he doesn't want care, I can't force myself on him."

Sophie hung up without saying good-bye. She pulled her things together and went for the second time to free Bill Crane.

Behind a curtain in the emergency room, he looked better than she'd expected. He was thin, but not disastrously so, and peacefully asleep. An ER doctor approached, and the nurse who had brought Sophie to the bedside retreated.

"Are you a relative of Mr. Crane's?"

"I'm his daughter."

"The good news is that he was just malnourished," he said, leading her away from Crane's bed as they talked. "He's getting some fluids now, and I expect he'll have some strength back before too long."

"That's wonderful."

"I understand that your father has elected to stop treatment for his cancer."

"Yes," she said. "To be honest, I just found this out myself. We're not really..."

But it had not been a question.

"These end-of-life issues are very difficult, Miss Crane. I don't blame him for making the decision. But the man hasn't eaten in two days. The kind of pain he's been in is entirely unnecessary. I'd recommend you get him into hospice after he's discharged."

"He doesn't want to go to hospice."

"I don't doubt that," the doctor said. "But if his family—if you—are going to leave him to starve in his apartment, then there aren't a lot of good options. Some palliative measures need to be taken. He can't be on his own at this point. And we can't keep him here if he doesn't want to be treated."

"My husband and I will take care of him."

"You're sure? It's going to be demanding."

"We're happy to do it. We didn't know how serious his condition was."

"All right. We'll move him upstairs in a few hours, but he should be up and about within a day or two. You can take him home then. We can have a hospital bed delivered. Insurance should cover that. And I can write some prescriptions for his pain. The most important thing is to make it as easy as possible."

He took Sophie's number and left her to wander back to where Crane lay sleeping. She sat down in the chair beside his bed. The pale green hospital gown had fallen from his shoulders, leaving his bony chest uncovered, and she saw the burn for the first time. It might have been two days old, instead of two decades. She reached to pull the gown over it, and it seemed fresh and warm to the touch. She felt the throb of blood, the struggle to live.

She could muster no outrage, even on Tom's behalf, only sadness as she thought of all that had been taken from him. He was her character now, and she looked upon him as God looks upon all the benighted. She imagined him writing letters to his son, letters never opened, pulled from between two bills in the mail pile and discarded by Beth before Tom ever saw them. She didn't know why she imagined this, since Beth was far too honest for such a thing. There had been no letters. But now there would be letters, for now it was up to her. She moved her hand from his burnt chest to his thin fingers, took them in her own, and cried. Anyone walking by would have thought them the dying father and grieving daughter she'd claimed them to be.

If Tom refused to take Bill in, she would stay downtown with him. But it wouldn't come to that. In the end, she was certain of Tom's goodness. She relied on it. Once he understood how helpless his father was, he would want to do this.

"Do you think he'll wake up soon?" Sophie asked a passing nurse.

"They're giving him something right now," the nurse said, glancing at his chart. She gestured to one of the two IV drips running into his arms. "He's going to be out for the rest of the day by the looks of it."

She might have left him there, taking the afternoon to make plans for bringing him home. But he had been entrusted to her. She bowed her head and prayed that he was not beyond saving.

His hand was still in hers when the darkness came, like a message announced. A full minute passed before the light returned with a loud hum and a commotion on the other side of the curtain that separated them from the world. Sophie stepped outside, where a nurse was calling the waiting room to attention.

"There's been an outage," she said. "The hospital is running on an emergency generator, and patient services shouldn't be affected. First of all, I need everyone to stay calm. In order to avoid confusion, we're asking that visitors say their good-byes and slowly make their way out to the street."

Sophie had no good-byes to say, so she left immediately. Outside in the early summer evening, with the sun still shining, it was difficult to tell that the power was gone until she saw the blank traffic lights and the pedestrians out in the street, directing cars while cabs on Seventh Avenue honked their horns.

She remembered blackouts from her childhood. They usually came after falling trees took down wires, and so coincided with violent storms. They were exciting, pitting her family against the elements without the usual advantage of technology. There was the romance of inhabiting a distant, candlelit time, summoning the natural resources of humanity. Their house was an old colonial in which every board squeaked, and on those evenings it seemed especially haunted by the past.

But now there had been no storm, and this wasn't supposed to happen in New York. Her parents had lived in the city during the blackout of the late seventies, before she was born. They had described it as a once-in-a-lifetime occurrence. Then again, their lifetimes had passed.

"Do you think?" a woman standing near Sophie asked, hinting at another attack on the still-raw city.

"No," the man beside her said. "Just an act of God."

When Sophie called Tom, a message told her that all circuits were busy. She thought of that morning two years earlier, struggling desperately for some contact with him. She tried again and received the same message. Then she headed uptown.

The lights were out in the storefronts along the avenue, and what shops had still been open were now closing. Everyone had left work, and the sidewalks were full. Some people seemed scared, but most already understood that nothing serious had happened. Two boys had climbed a streetlight on the corner, and they were perched together on it precariously, watching the chaos just below. People were already constructing the stories they would tell about the night of the big blackout. They started singing and celebrating, as if to live up to tomorrow's legend.

Sophie practiced the speech she would make to Tom that night. She wouldn't say anything about saving his father's soul. She would just say that they had an obligation. Tom understood well the language of oughts. She might add that caring for the man would be a way of proving that his father had no hold over him, that he had control over what kind of person he was.

The walk from the hospital took two hours, and night fell before she arrived home. Then came the walk up twenty-eight flights. Candles had been set down on every landing, bathing the stairwell in uneven light. Sophie thought again of the blackouts at home, remembering the bad storms, when days might pass before the lights went back on. She remembered how quickly it all became tiresome. You wanted to watch TV, to use appliances, to open the fridge. You wanted the ghosts to go away.

She opened the door and found Tom. He'd bought candles, which she hadn't thought to do, and set them along the kitchen counter and around the living room. Most remained unlit.

"I thought you'd be here," he said, when she walked in. Sophie tried to determine, in the flickering light, if there was a look of relief on his face.

"I know. I'm sorry."

Indeed, she was sorry. She was happy to see her husband, and she stepped over to him, putting her arms around his neck while he remained unmoving.

"Are you ever here when you say you are during the day?"

She hadn't told him anything yet, but he knew enough to be angry. Things were already out of her control.

"Of course I'm here. Where would I be?"

Then she saw her notebook in his hand, being waved like a weapon.

"With him."

"None of that came from him," she said. "I made all that up."

She knew this wouldn't help.

"So you were writing a story about it?"

"I don't know," she admitted. "I don't think so. I don't think I was really going to show it to anyone. This was just my way of making sense of things. You have to trust me."

"Then where were you today?"

Now she swept into action, sharing with him their new burden, which she'd carried all these blocks uptown.

"I got a call from the hospital, and I didn't have any choice. He's very sick. He can't live on his own anymore.

What he did to you was terrible, maybe unforgivable. But you don't have to forgive him to help him. We're the only family he has, and he needs us very badly. So I told the doctors we would take care of him. He only has a few weeks to live, I think. And I know you'll feel better for having done this. Although you won't really have to *do* anything. You just need to let me do it."

She continued on like this, not sure where the words were coming from. None of it bore any relation to the measured speech she'd prepared on her walk uptown. That script had been lost. Finally, she stopped and waited for something to register on Tom's blank face.

"You were with him today?"

He was no longer angry. He seemed confused, almost deflated.

"You never answer the phone," he said. "You're not here when you say you'll be."

As he spoke, it came to her.

"Why did you go through my notebook? You've never done that before in all these years."

He looked at it in his hands as if unsure how it had arrived there. Then he set it down on her desk like something fragile.

"I thought you'd started seeing someone."

She almost laughed in relief. It would all be so simple to clear up.

"Oh, Tom. But that's silly. I would never."

"It's not silly," he said. "People do it all the time."

How badly they had misunderstood each other, perhaps from the very beginning.

She was a summer at the firm. In a few more weeks she'd be returning to Charlottesville to finish law school. He wasn't sure that they would be together when she came back to New York in the spring, but she'd made him realize that he needed to live on his own for a while.

"I guess I've never really done that," he said, as if Sophie had deprived him of the chance.

"All right," Sophie said.

"All right?"

"What do you want me to say?"

"I thought you might raise your voice for once."

"Fuck you." She said it quietly. Not out of spite—it was just the way she talked.

A bag had been packed. How far in advance this had been done was not disclosed. Tom didn't say he was going to stay with the girl, but he didn't say otherwise. He might already have had an apartment somewhere.

"You owe me more than just walking out like this," Sophie said, though she wasn't sure he owed her anything. Anyway she didn't want him to stay and explain himself. If he was going, she wanted him to leave. There would be time for endless talk if talk was deemed necessary. All of that could come later. She had walked a long way, and she was exhausted now.

When she looked him over, duffel bag in hand, standing proud and afraid like a child, a great surprising store of love and goodwill and pity took over her heart. She thought of him waiting all day with this news in his gut, wondering where she was.

After he was gone, she lit the rest of the candles, turning the kitchen counter into an altar. Sister Dymphna, the nun who ran the classes for initiates, had said that God was like electricity. We couldn't see Him, most of us couldn't understand Him, but we knew we needed Him and we knew—indirectly, from His works—that He was always there.

When the urge for a cigarette came, she walked instinctively out on the deck, though now there was nothing stopping her from smoking inside. The only lights she saw below were from the cars. Sophie imagined living according to the rhythms of natural light. When the sun set, the day was done. Such a time seemed very far away. She looked up, expecting to see the usual empty New York sky. Instead she saw stars, and she thought of home. She thought of the Old Manse. The heavens were full of light, and seeing it she was herself illuminated by a shiver of dumb wonder.

7

THE NEXT MORNING *The Third Man* was back on the screen, and Max was back on the couch. Beside the over-filled ashtray on the table in front of him sat a cocktail glass whose contents might have been Max's breakfast or left over from the night before.

"You're making progress," I said.

"Progress is a self-serving bourgeois myth."

We were quiet then, watching Harry Lime run through the Viennese sewers.

"The cuckoo clock," I said eventually.

"The cuckoo clock," Max agreed.

Sophie had always been an early riser, and she'd gone to bed hours before we had, but the morning was mostly over before she came down. She still looked tired, standing beside the couch, smoking one of Max's cigarettes and reconciling herself to the new day.

"Hungry?" she asked me eventually.

We left Max with his movie and walked together to a diner on Waverly, where Sophie slumped across from me in the booth. Some unraveling had taken place since her arrival, or else she had all along been unraveled and I was only gradually recognizing it.

"I'm not sure I'm cut out for this lifestyle of yours," she said.

"Me neither," I told her. "No one is, really."

When we'd finished our lunch, Sophie led us west on Waverly toward Christopher, away from the house.

"You don't mind?" she asked. "I don't want to keep you from your writing."

She seemed to know well enough that she wasn't keeping me from anything. I hadn't done any work on the follow-up in weeks. It was tough to say what I'd been doing with my time before Sophie's arrival. I didn't even take these long walks anymore. Everything I passed on the street conspired to make my life inconsequential. Whatever reinvigorating force I needed couldn't be found there. Whenever I joked with Max about some bit of pop culture detritus that he had addressed with professional seriousness in the pages of his magazine, he quoted Schiller: *A man must be a good citizen of his age, as well as of his country.* I wasn't much of a citizen of either. In fact, it had become difficult even to step outside without a high-grade case of the late-capitalist heebie-jeebies. But as I turned up Seventh Avenue with Sophie, I didn't feel so ill-suited to the world.

"This is where I was when the lights went out," she said at Twelfth Street.

"At the hospital?"

"Getting Crane."

The blackout had happened only a few months before. I hadn't really placed Crane's story in time and it unsettled me to feel it creeping up on us. Sophie described that day as we continued uptown from St. Vincent's. We were in

Chelsea before I realized that we were retracing the walk to her apartment. We crossed town along the bottom of Central Park, where the sidewalk was crowded with vendors, caricaturists, street-corner singers, and the tourists for whom they all existed.

This was near the neighborhood where I'd grown up, where my mother still lived. I'd known that Sophie was living there, that she'd been going to the church my family had once attended. But I wasn't sure exactly where her apartment was, so I didn't know how far from it we were when I spotted Tom. He was half a block away and heading toward us. I hadn't seen him for years, and to my eyes he had grown fat and satisfied. He had his arm around a small, smiling blonde, the kind of cute New Hampton girl he should have been with all along. If this was the girl, she would have gone back to law school by then, which meant that she had come up to visit him. Otherwise Tom was already on to someone else, exercising his new freedom.

I noticed him before Sophie did, and I had time to say something or gracefully guide us across the street. But I did nothing. I wanted Tom to see us together. I liked the symmetry of the four of us coming face to face. It put me in the same category as this girl who'd broken up their marriage. And I thought it might be good for Sophie to have me there when she encountered Tom, as she would have to eventually.

The girl looked up at us, and she knew. Somehow, through a whispered word or a stiffening of her body, she communicated the knowledge to Tom, who also looked up the block. Only Sophie remained unaware of what was coming.

"Tom," I said quietly when they were about ten feet away, as much warning Sophie as greeting him.

"Charlie Blakeman," Tom said suspiciously, as though I were an old friend whose sudden appearance with his estranged wife constituted a betrayal. I was reminded how little I actually knew Tom. We'd spoken only a few times in four years of college together, and after that he was just the boyfriend, and then the husband, of the girl I loved. I'd known nothing before that week of the details of his life, the circumstances of his childhood. Now that I did, I wasn't sure what to do with these facts. Nothing about his appearance had ever seemed informed by tragedy. I felt something I hadn't felt even after first discovering that Sophie had chosen him: I hated Tom. It was a relief to see that he and Sophie couldn't even look at each other.

"What brings you to this neighborhood?" he asked, as though the answer weren't standing next to me.

"Just on a walk," I said. "This may be the last good walking day we'll get for a while."

"You never know," Tom answered. "Some things hang around longer than we expect."

We all waited for him to introduce the girl. When he didn't, she offered her hand to me and said, "I'm Willa."

"I'm Charlie. I went to college with Tom."

She turned to Sophie, who had been watching all this without a word but now extended her hand and smiled.

"I'm Sophie," she said. "I'm your boyfriend's wife."

"We have to run," Tom said then, still addressing only me. "I'm sorry to be rude, but we're in a rush."

Then they were gone. The whole thing had taken only a moment. I waited to see what Sophie would make of this encounter.

"After he left," she said, "I went out on the deck and looked up at the stars. I couldn't remember the last time I'd seen them."

"Me neither."

"It just happened, though. The disappearance of the stars, I mean. Not in our lifetime, maybe, but within a few generations. We don't think that much about it, but we're historically unprecedented. Standing out there, I imagined that the whole world was lit up like a city, so that no one ever saw the stars. It's going to happen eventually. What will people make of us then, and all our talk about the heavens? Songs about constellations. Stargazing poetry."

I felt obliged to play along.

"'How countlessly they congregate,'" I said. "'O'er our tumultuous snow.'"

"'His heart was darker than the starless night,'" Sophie said. "What will that mean once every night is starless? They'll think we all suffered some mass delusion."

"Or else they'll know we saw something they can't see anymore."

"Even worse."

Predictably, Max and I had used the blackout as an occasion for a party. We'd gone to Gerhard's roof and looked out at the darkened city. But I didn't remember anyone looking up at the stars or thinking anything about them.

"Maybe they won't be bothered by it," I said. "They'll get the convenience of cities, the survival of mankind. That will be worth the disappearance."

"How will they know it was worth it, if they've never seen the stars? How could they measure their loss beneath an empty sky?"

I didn't know how to answer this.

"What happened next?" I asked.

"What do you mean?"

"After you stepped back inside and forgot about the stars."

"I went downtown to save Crane's soul."

It started to rain before we arrived at Sophie's building. Not a clear-skied summer rain, but heavy from charcoal clouds. The wind picked up, knocking over a trash can on the corner, spilling paper and coffee cups into the gutter. I hailed a cab and we took it back to Gerhard's. We were both soaking wet, and Sophie's hair, longer than I had ever seen it, was pressed against her face.

"I should go home," she said. "I've imposed on you and Max long enough."

We both knew that her presence was the opposite of an imposition.

"Some visitors stay for months," I said.

"Well, I'm not that sort."

"You haven't finished your story," I said.

"I've told you enough."

The cab pulled up outside Gerhard's, and I paid the driver. Sophie pulled me close and pressed her wet face to mine. I didn't understand what was happening. I stepped from the cab and waited for her to follow me out. Then the door closed, and she was gone. I hadn't heard her say anything to the driver, and I didn't know where he was taking her. I was too surprised to do anything but stand in the rain, watching her go.

Inside, Max sat watching his movie. It might have been his second time through since we'd left, or his third.

"Beware the pathetic fallacy," he said, when he saw me dripping in the doorway. "Attend to the weather in your heart."

I went upstairs without answering, to shower and change. By the time I was done, the rain had passed. I stood for a while at my bedroom window, looking out at the empty sky. Downstairs, the television was off. Max was staring at the blank screen with a fresh drink in his hand.

"Do you want one?" he asked.

"Sure."

"Where's Sophie?"

The question came as a relief. At least it confirmed that she'd been there, that I hadn't made the whole thing up.

"She left," I said.

"For good?"

"We ran into Tom and his new girl on the street, but I'm not sure if that's what made her leave."

"I don't think she was ever planning to stay for more than a few days."

"What makes you say that?"

He let out an annoyed hiss of breath, as if sensing a gathering complication.

"That's what she said when she called."

"She called? I thought you ran into her on the street."

"She called me at work a few days before she showed up. She wanted to know if she could come for a visit."

"Why didn't you tell me this?"

"She asked me not to. And anyway I knew you'd drive yourself crazy. I told her we'd be having some people over on Friday, and she could come then if she wanted. I have no idea why she would lie to you about that."

"Just out of nowhere, she called you up and said she wanted to visit?"

"She wanted to come into the city for a few days."

"Did she say she wanted to visit, or did she say she wanted to come into the city?"

"I don't know, Charlie. It was a phone conversation. I didn't bring out my hermeneutic toolkit."

"I'm not looking for an exegesis," I said. "I just want to know what she told you."

"Well, if there isn't going to be an exegesis, then I don't see why we need to establish an authoritative text."

"Max," I said. "Help me out here."

He set his drink down on the table as though I'd spoiled it.

"She wanted to stay a few days."

"Did she say where she'd been staying until then?"

"We didn't really get into anything like that."

He seemed to be making things more mysterious than they needed to be.

"Was something going on between the two of you?"

"You mean eight years ago? Or this week?"

"Where did you guys go when you left the party that night she showed up?"

"Jesus Christ, Charlie. The perpetual-adolescent thing is not without its charm. But we're not *actually* still eighteen years old."

"I'm just asking."

"We went outside and took a lap around the park. She wanted to talk, about you. How you were doing, whether you were seeing anyone. How your writing was going. I don't know why she didn't ask you this herself."

"She asked about my writing?"

"So she did."

"What did you tell her?"

"I said you were working on a few things. Frankly, I wasn't sure that having Sophie Wilder take a sudden interest in your life was much good for anyone. Which seems like sound reasoning in retrospect. But I kept my mouth shut. When you got to the party, she kind of flipped out, so we went for a walk. And then we got back inside, and you had gone upstairs. Does that satisfy you?"

"Sure," I said, though we both knew that it could not.
Max stood and headed for the kitchen.
"Let me get you that drink."

In the days that followed I came to wish that Sophie had never returned to my life. Not that I'd been particularly happy, but I had been comfortable enough in my unhappiness. I'd made some peace with it. Now that peace was gone. Her presence in my life—even as a shadow—was a challenge. It had always been a challenge, I realized. A great effort was required to meet that challenge, and I didn't know that I still had it in me to make that effort.

This challenge was complicated by the discovery that Sophie had planned her visit. What else had she planned? She might have known that Tom would be in their old neighborhood, dropping off a key or performing some other scheduled task. Countless chance encounters that marked our history might have been matters of Sophie's design.

What was she after, then? Why had she designed things this one way instead of any other? Why had she come when she did, and, having come back, why did she leave so abruptly? It would have cost her nothing to come inside, pack up the few things she'd brought, and say a proper good-bye.

I didn't know where to begin to find her. We had fallen that far apart. I didn't have her cell phone number or a recent e-mail address. She'd said she was going home, but I wasn't sure what that meant. I found a listing for Sophie and Tom in the phone book, but I knew they weren't living in the apartment. I called anyway and let it ring. I sent an e-mail to her old New Hampton alumni account, though I rarely checked my own and when I did it was filled with spam. I wrote that it had been great to see her. That I'd love to talk with her again, and she should let me know the next time she was in the neighborhood. I didn't express any urgency, but she would understand if she ever got the e-mail. After I'd finished, I felt the helplessness that always comes after sending a message to which one desperately wants an immediate reply. There was nothing left to do.

A few days later I went for a walk, hoping to recapture the habit I'd lost before Sophie's arrival. Music played from three directions in Washington Square. A three-piece jazz band—drums and a horn and a stand-up bass, all of the players probably students at the university—had attracted a large crowd to the park's south end. Beneath the arch on the north side a desperate-looking man played a slow version of the Beatles' "I Should Have Known Better" on an acoustic guitar. In the western part of the park a boom box played, surrounded by the same group that had been dancing the week before. Only the eastern end was open, and I went out that way.

I didn't quite mean to repeat the first walk I'd taken with Sophie, but that's what I did. Everything fell into place when I reached Crane's block. She'd been leading me there all along. This is where her story ended. And I realized why she'd left when she had: she'd told me everything she could.

For a long time I stared at his building, as if it might give up its secrets through the force of my will. I'd almost laughed when she told me that she'd gone to save his soul. I couldn't quite take it seriously. I'd been raised more or less Catholic myself, gone to Catholic school my whole life before arriving at New Hampton, but I don't think I knew a single person who would have spoken in that way about saving someone's soul. The religious people I knew talked about their faith apologetically. It was an embarrassment to their own reason and intelligence, but somehow a necessary one. Their justifications often suggested something vaguely therapeutic. They needed a sense of meaning in their lives. They wanted to believe that things happened for a reason. To speak of souls and damnation, to speak of intervening in another life for the sake of salvation, was beyond all this.

When it had finally become clear that Sophie's trips to the church off campus were neither rumor nor research, that something had changed for her, I thought of her pregnancy and my failure to help her. Then I thought of her joining us at midnight mass for three Christmases, which so far as I knew were the first three times she'd been to a Catholic church. I couldn't help relating her new behavior to me. I did so again when I heard that she'd started going to St. Agnes, the same church I'd brought her to then, though it was also the closest one to her apartment. We'd never spoken about any of this during our few conversations over the years. I didn't ask questions about her religion, since her answers would only mark out the distance between us. Mostly it didn't seem real to me. I still pictured Sophie as I'd always known her, and I couldn't imagine that person turning to God at a time of need.

My own father came from a long line of believers, though he wasn't much of one himself. For my mother it was all a matter of indifference. She didn't object to my being baptized and confirmed, but she didn't pretend for a moment it meant anything to her. And whatever talent I had for faith had died along with my father. But my mother and I had continued going to church a few times a year with family, and I could understand religion as an inheritance, a family tradition.

I understood it also as an aesthetic choice. I'd spent enough time around churches in my childhood to appreciate the pull of certain ceremonies, the dark medieval appeal of incense in the nose. It seemed a fair response to the chaos of the modern world. That kind of religion was always an option for a certain sensibility. And there was religion as bohemian provocation or performance. Dylan born again. It wouldn't have been so surprising if Max one day announced that he'd found God, as a kind of affectation, like playing bridge with retirees at the card clubs uptown.

But when Sophie spoke about saving Crane's soul, I saw that her faith had nothing to do with sensibility. She believed. Another challenge: I hadn't thought such a thing was still possible.

That night I opened a notebook at my desk. It was the old marble kind that we both used to use, and a few pages were already filled with false starts from months before. I ripped those out and threw them away, so that I could start fresh. I found a pencil in the drawer and chewed on it while examining the page. I had gnawed down to the lead when Morgan Bench appeared in the doorway of my room.

"Hey man," he said, "have you got any smokes? We're all out downstairs and no one feels like going to the corner."

"There should be some on the dresser," I told him without looking up from the page.

"Cool," he said. He stayed in the doorway. "What are you getting up to in here?"

"Writing," I said.

"Working on the follow-up?"

"Tough to say."

"I hear you." He had found the cigarettes by then and lit one. "How's that going?"

"Not great," I told him. "It's kind of tough to concentrate in this environment."

"Right on," said Morgan. "Fucking George Bush, you know?"

"I was speaking more about the *local* environment."

"Well, all politics is local, right?"

I watched Morgan turn down the hall and head for the stairs before rising to go after him. "Wait up," I said. "I'm due for a break."

The next morning I came down late and Max was back in front of the screen, watching something in black and white I'd never seen before.

"A letter came for you," he said, as though this were a regular occurrence.

"A letter?"

"It's on the table by the door."

The envelope had no return address, but the handwriting on the front was unmistakably hers. I opened it and found a single sheet of lined paper.

Dear Charlie, the letter began. *Please excuse the anachronistic method of communication, which isn't entirely an affectation. I'm staying at the Old Manse, where there's no internet connection. There is a phone, of course, but this is only half a help, without a number to call.*

The Old Manse was our ironic name, after Hawthorne and Emerson, for the house where Sophie had grown up in Connecticut. It was left to her after her parents died, and I'd been there a few times while we were in school. There had been enough in the estate to pay taxes on the house and keep it inhabitable, but Sophie had often spoken in college of selling it after graduation, so she'd have something to live on while she wrote. I'd assumed it had long ago left her hands. But once she'd published her first book and married a man with a career, it would have made sense to hold on to the place. I should have guessed that Sophie would be staying there, that this is what she would have meant by going home.

I'm writing this on Tuesday. If you get it in time to make the one thirty train on Friday, I'll be waiting at the station. Of course I'll understand if you don't appear.

"What day is it today?" I asked Max.

"You've got all the tough questions," he said before checking his phone. "It's Friday."

"And how about the time?"

"Just after noon."

I barely waited to read the rest of the letter. There wasn't much to it. She had signed her name in all lower-case: *yrs, sophie.* Underneath, a few lines down, so that I almost missed it, a postscript:

At night here, you can always see the stars.

PART TWO
The Law Within

1

ON THE THIRD day, they told Sophie to pick her father up. She hadn't been back to the hospital before then. She'd thought she would take the time to prepare, but her preparations had finally amounted to sitting in the apartment, wondering what came next. She had decided to stay downtown with Crane—it made no sense to bring him to this place, strange to him and no longer home to her—but she'd done no packing before the call came.

Now she gathered her things as though for a trip. She meant to stay as long as he survived, but she didn't know how long that would be, if she'd committed herself to days or to months. She packed a week's worth of clothes, along with toothpaste and shampoo, her makeup kit and an expensive face cream that Tom had bought her for her birthday the year before. She realized the foolishness of packing these last two items, but she knew that if she left them now she would be leaving them for good.

The only book she packed was the King James Bible from the shelf near her desk. She'd bought it at the college store on the day she returned to campus from Christmas at Beth's. She'd never read the Bible before in any version. It was a strange thing to recognize about herself. Countless things she'd read alluded to it, and she had some sense of understanding these allusions. But she didn't know the book.

Because she understood the Book of Job to be the most "literary" of them, she'd begun there. She was amazed by Satan's challenge to God, that he test Job with misfortune: *Put forth thine hand now, and touch all that he hath, and he will curse thee to thy face.* But more amazing still had been God's acceptance of the challenge: *All that he hath is in thy power.* By the time she got to Job's lament—*Why died I not from the womb? why did I not give up the ghost when I came out of the belly? Why did the knees prevent me? or why the breasts that I should suck? For now should I have lain still and been quiet, I should have slept*—she was weeping in her room.

If she'd not read those words in her dorm room that day, the experience at Beth's church might have become an odd memory, rather than the thing that changed her life. As she sat weeping, she thought of the child she'd lost. She knew she would have ended the pregnancy in any case, but as it was she'd never had the choice. There had been two days of terrible cramps, at the end of which she'd gone to the infirmary. That had been a month before fall break, a month before Tom sat down at the table beside her. She had not taken time since then to measure the loss. I should have lain still and been quiet, she thought. I should have slept.

The Bible was the last thing she packed before leaving the apartment, leaving her old life forever. She would return, but it would never again be home. Their lease would be up in the fall. She and Tom would each find a place to stay. She didn't know what would come then. She knew only what came now, which was Bill Crane.

At the hospital, he stood with only slight help from a cane, looking much as he had when they had first met in that same place weeks before. His appearance struck Sophie in the way of a resurrection. Having seen him unconscious in bed, tubes running into his nose and arms, she'd vaguely imagined caring for a mute, unmoving object. But he was still very much alive. Not that he looked good. He was even thinner than he'd been. His shirt hung loose from his body like a kind of smock. His belt cinched his black pants, which looked like an empty trash bag pulled tight at the top. On a street corner or a bench in Union Square, he would easily have been taken for a vagrant.

"Your father's a little disoriented now," the doctor said. He pulled Sophie out of Crane's hearing range, but close enough for him to look on helplessly as they conferred. "He was actually quite lucid earlier today. That will be in and out, I imagine. As the malignancy spreads, there's likely to be slippage as far as cognition goes. Try to keep talking with him, keep him engaged, even when he isn't saying much or doesn't seem to be picking things up."

He continued in this way, telling Sophie what to expect, making no effort to sound encouraging. They would send someone from hospice care to the apartment the next day, to bring supplies and to show her what else was required.

"Is your husband a strong man?"

She nearly laughed.

"In his way," she said.

"He may need to do some heavy lifting. Once your father is immobile, you'll want to keep moving him to avoid bedsores."

"I think we're strong enough for that."

"The biggest challenge from here will be managing the pain."

Isn't it always, Sophie thought.

"This is fairly heavy-duty stuff I'm giving you," the doctor said as he handed Sophie two prescription sheets. "One is for pain and the other is to help him sleep. Read all the directions and administer them carefully."

"And these will make it better?"

"Not entirely. So long as he's alive, he's going to be suffering."

Two orderlies put Crane in a wheelchair, though he was moving well enough with the cane. It was hard to tell if he'd understood the arrangements being made, if he expected her to leave after dropping him off as she had the last time. She couldn't be sure he even connected her to the woman who had taken him home before. *Keep him engaged*, Sophie thought, pushing him out to the street. How did you engage a man as you took him home to die?

"They said you're my daughter," Crane announced.

"It was less complicated that way," Sophie said.

"You're not my daughter."

"I know."

They didn't talk much after that until they got inside his building, where she looked up the stairs and understood the enormity of what she'd taken on. At the hospital the talk of washing and changing, bedpans and sponge baths, had not seemed real. But the steps in front of them now were the great challenge of her life.

"I can manage this," he said as he rose from the chair.

So he did, gripping the railing with one hand and his cane with the other. She walked a few steps behind, dragging the wheelchair while pressing a useless, encouraging shoulder to the small of his back. If he lost his balance, she knew, he'd take them both down.

She unfolded the wheelchair as he unlocked the door, but he ignored it and made for the couch.

"I'm going to fill these prescriptions and do some shopping," she said. "Is there anything in particular you want?"

He looked at her blankly, as if to say, What could I possibly want?

"By way of food, I mean."

The doctor had given her the name of a protein drink and suggested she stock up, adding that he could eat small amounts of solid food if he had the appetite for it. Nuts were particularly good. But he was beyond the doctor's care; she would give him whatever he wanted.

"I'm not really hungry," he told her. "I've been having stomach troubles."

If he was making a joke, he gave no sign of it.

"So I've heard."

On her way back into the building, she passed Lucia Ortiz's door, and she considered knocking to let Lucia know that she had done the thing she should have done long before: come to care for her father. She walked by, comforted just to know that the woman was there. When she arrived upstairs, Crane seemed more present, as though some part of him that had been earlier asleep had come awake in her absence.

Sophie heated a bowl of soup that she hoped they could share. She poured a can of the protein drink into a glass she found in the sink and filled a small bowl with unsalted cashews. She returned to the other room, where she sat down beside him on the couch. When she handed him the glass, he examined it like an insult before placing it on the table in front of them.

"How do you feel?" Sophie asked.

"About the same."

They sat in silence while she ate the soup and thought about how hard it all would be. When she had finished, she set the bowl down beside the full glass. She wanted to tell him what she knew, what she had learned about his life since the last time she was in this apartment. She looked at him, trying to determine how the knowledge had changed him in her eyes.

"I can read to you, if you'd like. It might pass the time."

He set his head down on the arm of the couch and closed his eyes, as though to say that her presence was a matter of indifference but that he wouldn't stop her from doing as she wished. She reached in her bag for the Bible.

She hadn't thought about what passages she might read to him. She wanted something from the New Testament, ideally from the Gospels, a message of redemption rather than damnation. She picked more or less at random from John and started to read.

"'Now Jesus loved Martha, and her sister, and Lazarus,'" Sophie read. "'When he had heard therefore that he was sick, he abode two days still in the same place where he was. Then after that saith he to his disciples, Let us go into Judaea again. His disciples say unto him, Master, the Jews of late sought to stone thee; and goest thou thither again? Jesus answered, Are there not twelve hours in the day? If any man walk in the day, he stumbleth not, because he seeth the light of this world. But if a man walk in the night, he stumbleth, because there is no light in him.'"

"Why are you reading me this?"

He'd been sitting so quietly that she'd doubted he was listening, or even awake. She'd nearly forgotten he was there. Now she saw how brutal it was to read such a passage to a dying man.

"I'm sorry," she said. "I wasn't thinking."

But this wasn't what had upset him.

"Don't start in with the Ivan Ilyich shit," he said. "There aren't going to be any Communion wafers or death-bed conversions."

"It wasn't anything like that."

"I'd bet I know that book a lot better than you do," Crane said. "And he's a fascist."

She thought he'd lost his sense again, had started slipping back away from her.

"King James?"

"God. The first totalitarian. Has to control everything. Reads your mail. Bugs your phone. Watches while you take a shit. I don't see what's to admire. And death camps. Auschwitz is a beach vacation compared to the circles of hell. You get sent there for the same reason, incidentally: for not being a Christian."

The shock she felt came not from his resistance, but from the idea that she'd thought it could be otherwise. After her conversion, Sophie had expected to have such conversations routinely with skeptical friends. But no one seemed interested in questioning her faith. Perhaps they didn't care. Or else they found belief so foreign as to be beyond discussion. For a time she'd undertaken a self-interrogation, seeing that no one else would do it for her. But now that it mattered, now that she was faced with one whom she wished to convince, her answers escaped her.

"You're oversimplifying," she said, aware how inadequate her response was. "He isn't spying in some prurient way. He's not trying to catch anyone at anything. And He doesn't control everything. He could, but He gives us free will."

"Free will," he almost roared, before slumping back into the couch. "You're free to do what you choose. And if you don't choose to worship me, I'll send you to the flames. I'd think better of it if He just made us do whatever He wanted, instead of leaving us to guess and burning us for guessing wrong."

The arguments weren't new to her. She'd read them before, even made them occasionally to herself. The case for a malevolent God was more compelling, if anything, than the case for no God at all. But it also seemed, once you'd accepted His existence as fact, difficult to question His nature.

"I don't fault you for being angry," Sophie said.

"Well that's a great relief," Crane told her. "I would hate to have that on my conscience."

"Of course I can't imagine what you've been through."

"You're right about that," he said. "So don't even try. I don't know what Tom told you, what you think you know about my life, but you don't know shit, so I don't want to hear about it."

For lack of anything else to do, she brought her empty bowl into the kitchen. When she returned to the couch, a dying man had replaced the enraged beast.

"Have some," she said, raising the glass of sludgy liquid.

"I don't want it."

She sat back down next to him.

"If you don't have anything, you're just going to waste away."

"That was the idea," he said. "I don't know why that woman from downstairs came checking up on me. She never took any interest before."

"I asked her to."

Crane looked at Sophie with a kind of begrudging respect, as at an adversary who had proven worthy of his best effort.

"You're the reason I'm still alive, then."

"I guess I am."

"It's nice to know who to blame."

She decided then that his anger was her best opportunity. Indifference would have been far more difficult to overturn.

"I only wanted to help you."

"You got me home, at least. So I'm back where I started, and you can go back to wherever you belong."

They hadn't told him, then.

"I'm staying," she said.

"For how long?"

Until you die, said the silence between them.

"For good."

"And Tom won't mind?"

"He's not really in a position to object."

"How's that?"

She had hoped not to talk about it, though of course that was impossible.

"He left."

"Also for good?"

"I don't know," she said reflexively. Then she considered the question and added, "I suppose so. It's not really the kind of relationship where we just come and go. And Tom doesn't make decisions lightly. I don't imagine he'd leave if it weren't for good."

He gave her a look somewhere between vindication and sympathy, urging her to elaborate, as though they were in league, the two whom Tom had abandoned. But she wanted no part of that storyline, having already lost interest in the predictable facts of her failed marriage.

"You should take these pills," she said. "One is for the pain, the other will help you sleep. But you can't take them on an empty stomach. You need to have some of that drink."

Crane took two sips and turned to her, needful. The desire to loosen pain's grip on him trumped even his willfulness, even his cruelty. It was a terrible thing to see. Better that he should rage.

After he took the pills, he rose by his own power from the couch. Sophie followed him to the bedroom, where he pulled off his shirt. She flinched at the sight of his pale and ruined body. The burn was larger than she'd first suspected, occupying all of one shoulder and arm and most of his chest. It was red and hashed and swollen and looked almost like something that had been draped over him, something that he might take off as a last preparation for bed. It extended down to his gut, where it touched with the fresh scar across his belly—the mangled meeting place that Crane had been reaching into his shirt to work over on the day they met. He sat still on the bed, seeming to present himself to her, as if to say: *This is what the world sets upon us.* But his face showed no intent. He hardly knew she was there.

She was no help to him, and she didn't want to watch him undress, but having followed him into the room she wasn't sure how to leave. Finally, he was down to his boxer shorts, and he pulled his legs up onto the bed. His clothes lay in a heap on the floor, like a body cast off by the spirit, and she left them there. She turned off the light and let him sleep.

In the kitchen she looked through the odds and ends she'd bought a few hours earlier—a few more cans of soup, two boxes of spaghetti, two jars of tomato sauce. She considered trying one of the protein drinks, if only to know what she was asking of Crane when she made him force down a few sips before handing over his pills. And then she spotted the bottle of scotch sitting in a dusty corner of the kitchen counter.

She'd taken her last drink the night before she found out she was pregnant. Only after the miscarriage had this struck her as odd, suggesting that some part of her had considered keeping the baby. By that time, she was glad she'd stopped; she didn't want anything to blame herself for. She might have started again, but she didn't. For a long time alcohol didn't appeal to her. Later, when she sometimes wanted a drink, inertia kept her from it. She was known around campus by then as both a religious convert and a reformed drinker, and so these facts were naturally linked in the minds of others, though she'd stopped drinking months before the first stirrings of her faith and the two things had nothing to do with each other. She'd never declared to herself or anyone else that she meant to quit; she'd just stopped, in a moment of choice.

All of which left her free to start again. Why she wanted a drink just then, as opposed to any other time, she couldn't say. But why should she keep herself from it, if she did? She poured a glass. The ice cube trays in the freezer were predictably empty, but she added some water from the sink. She took her first sip while still standing in the kitchen. She coughed and added more water to the glass, which she took back to the living room.

"It's not my Irish," she said out loud. "But it's something."

On the coffee table in front of the couch sat Crane's pack of cigarettes. She lit one to complete the picture and took a single drag before leaving it to burn in the ashtray. She picked up the Bible from the table and began leafing through it.

At the time she'd bought it, she'd known in an academic way that it was a Protestant Bible, but she hadn't thought much about this until speaking with Father Edmundson, the pastor of the church in New Hampton.

She didn't know why she hadn't gone to the chapel on campus. It wasn't embarrassment that kept her away. Plenty of students went to mass in town, and she was aware that some spoke about her attendance. She supposed she had not wanted to be treated by the school's chaplain as some late adolescent going through a religious phase. She was sure that it was more than that.

After a few weeks, she'd introduced herself to Father Edmundson and tried to describe what had happened to her.

"Do you read the Bible?" he'd asked during their second or third conversation.

She'd told him about the copy she'd bought.

"If you're going to think about this, you might try the Revised Standard version."

She'd gone out and bought the recommended translation, and often studied it. But she still returned to that King James translation. It felt truer to her in its beauty, closer to God's real voice, though sometimes she worried that this preference suggested her faith was more literary than spiritual.

A few weeks later, Father Edmundson recommended that she buy a copy of the Catechism.

"I don't tell everyone to do that," he said. "But it seems like it might have some impact on you."

"How can we speak about God?" one section was titled. "Since our knowledge of God is limited," it read, "our language about him is equally so." The section went on to speak about language's limits, its inability to capture God in His "infinite simplicity." Reading those two words, she felt again the stirring she'd felt on Christmas day. She realized that all the words she was reading about God had value as approximations only because she had stood in direct, ineffable contact with that infinite simplicity.

Father Edmundson made no effort to pressure her in her studies. If anything he treated her fervor with doubt. But when she continued attending mass and speaking to him about what she was learning, he enrolled her in the church's Rite of Christian Initiation for Adults program. It was springtime then, and he said that if all went well she might be baptized the following Easter.

That night she told Tom about her decision. He was the first to know, really, since talking to the priest didn't precisely count as talking to a person. Tom had seemed happy enough when she'd started attending mass with him, but he found it curious that she went alone on the weeks when he was too busy with schoolwork. Now he looked baffled.

"You don't have to do it," he said.

She both did and did not have to, it seemed to her. Either way his response was unexpected.

"What do you mean?"

"I mean, you don't have to do it for me."

"Of course I wouldn't do it for you."

"Oh," he said. "I'd thought you might."

She would come in the years that followed to cultivate an image of driving her parents' old Jaguar to ask Beth to be her sponsor. She would remember the smile on Beth's face, the joy shared between them in that moment. But she'd willfully set aside from those memories the fact that she'd originally meant to ask Tom. She'd set aside the night spent crying, thinking of that response that had stopped her short. *You don't have to do it.* His real meaning had eventually become clear: Tom didn't want her to be more like him and Beth, to ground herself in the soil of his life. He wanted instead to join her in unrootedness.

Another forgotten disappointment returned to her now as she sat on Crane's couch: Tom didn't understand why they couldn't keep sleeping together.

"It's a sin," she'd said, still trying the word on her tongue.

"But it was all right before?"

"I wasn't Catholic before."

"But I was."

"That wasn't my concern."

"So you're saying that what we were doing was wrong, and you just didn't know any better?"

She hadn't been sure she was saying that.

"I'm not sure I'm saying that."

It hurt him that she could even consider it this way. It hurt her, too, in fact. She didn't know how to relate to the person she had been, a person who seemed still to exist and to follow her at times, asserting some claim. It wasn't as easy for her as it seemed to be for the converts she'd read about. She couldn't toss off her old life so easily. At the same time, the laws of the Church, set down by men descended in a direct line from the apostles, seemed the closest access one could have to the infinite simplicity. It was the only path she had thus far been shown.

Tom had been ready to leave for a time. And why not? They hadn't been seeing each other all that long; there was no reason their lives should already be decided, no reason that Sophie's new faith should bring them together rather than divide them. Sophie had known all along that Tom had no great religious feelings himself, that it mattered to him only because it mattered to Beth. But her conversion was bound up in her mind with meeting Tom, and the change in her life seemed fundamentally to include him.

In the end, he hadn't left. But his patience had limits, and their early marriage was related to the line she'd drawn. Like a character from an old novel, he had proposed in order to get the thing he wanted, to possess her entirely. It hadn't bothered Sophie to know this. They would have married eventually. What difference did it make if they did it sooner than their friends, who would spend their twenties living together, doing everything but taking a vow?

So she had told herself then. But it all struck her differently now that Tom was gone. Now that he'd told her: I never really got the chance to live on my own. As if she had forced him to make this choice. You were the one who couldn't wait, she would have said, if he were there to hear it.

Sophie set the Bible back on the table and looked down. On the floor, partially hidden beneath the couch, was one of the manila folders that had been everywhere on her first visit, the ones she had tried to neaten up but that always appeared again spread out on the floor and the couch. She reached for it, intending only to set it somewhere, to straighten the place out a bit. But she no longer owed anyone her discretion, and once it was in her hand it was impossible not to open it.

Inside was a thick stack of yellowed newspaper clippings. They seemed to be mostly from the early nineties, and they didn't mean much to Sophie. When she closed the folder, she saw the number seven written on the front of it. The rest of the folders, lodged under the table and the couch, had numbers on them, too. It took her a few minutes of searching to find number one. It also contained newspaper clips, from a paper called the *Columbia Daily Tribune*. On the top of the pile was a small item, a few paragraphs taking up less than one column, beneath the headline "Columbia Woman Dies in Fire Near Fort Leonardwood." Beneath the headline it read: "Son, UM Professor Husband, Survive." The paper was dated August 13, 1983. The source of the fire, the article said, was unknown, but no mention was made of any suspicions about the cause. It was reported that William Crane, a professor at Missouri, was in critical condition, struggling for his life.

It appeared that his injuries were sustained while searching in the burning house for his son. The police were calling the man a hero.

Who would start a fire and then run inside to save someone from it? She had seen the scars, so at least that part of the story was likely true. Why hadn't Tom mentioned that his father had saved him? Why would he not let even that act be counted in the ledger on Crane's behalf?

For it did count. That Crane had kept these clippings so close at hand for twenty years counted for something also, though she couldn't say for what. Each time she put the folders away, they had reappeared. She imagined Crane spending his days going over these clippings, thinking about what had happened. It was a terrible thing to envision. She set the page aside and looked at the one that followed it in the pile. "Police Investigating Fort Leonardwood Fire," the headline said. The words below she read several times before they meant anything to her: "Autopsy Reveals Victim Pregnant."

The information settled slowly, and much had to shift in accommodating it. The words that Crane had spoken outside the hospital came to her: *You're not my daughter.* Had there been a daughter, she would have been much younger than Sophie, just twenty now, perhaps a junior in college. Tom would have been old enough at the time to be told that he would have a sister. It just depended on how far along the pregnancy was at the time of the fire.

Every sheet in this pile, and in the other folders throughout the room, held the threat of such awful revelations. Bill Crane's whole story was in the apartment, waiting to be read. He had even put it in numbered order. And the story began just where one might have thought it had ended. The idea terrified and captivated Sophie. She closed the folder and slid it out of sight.

The cigarette, burned most of the way down, had gone out in the ashtray. She lit another and smoked it while finishing her drink. Then she stood without thinking to refill her glass. How much is lost, she thought. As she finished her next drink, she thought about the night ahead. The couch was large enough to fit her spread out between its arms. She could have looked for a blanket or a pillow somewhere in Crane's room, but she couldn't bear to go back in. If she got cold, she would take more clothes from her bag. She turned out the lights and lay down in the darkness of this new life.

2

I LEFT FOR the Manse without knowing how long I'd been invited to stay. Sophie could have asked me to come away forever, to abandon Gerhard's house and everything in it, and I would have done so without a thought. But I didn't want to arrive packed for a week if she expected me for an afternoon. So I threw a single change of clothes and two books into a small duffel bag. I also packed the few things she'd left behind when she'd sped off in the cab.

Sophie waited at the station in the driver's seat of her parents' old Jaguar. I'd forgotten about this car, which she'd had on campus when we were at school. It must have been at least twenty-five years old. I spotted it before leaving the train, but I waited a moment on the platform, pretending confusion while I calmed myself. She flashed the brights to let me know she was there.

"It still runs," I said by way of greeting.

"When all else collapses."

We'd been eighteen, driving from New Hampton to New York, when Sophie told me that car was keeping her parents alive. She'd meant it seriously. Throughout most of her childhood it was the family's only car. But a few months before the crash her father had bought a new one, which he'd been driving that night. Because it was so new, it was easily forgotten. Afterward, Sophie would see the Jag in the driveway and think: *They can't be dead; the car is right here.* She would go outside in the middle of the night and run her hands over the body, feeling its solidity. No dents, no scratches. They're asleep upstairs, she would tell herself. I've had a bad dream.

She wasn't much given to mysticism, at least in those days, but something in her believed that her parents were safe somewhere so long as the car was okay. At the same time, she rejected this magical thinking, wanted to unburden herself of it, so she made shows of carelessness toward the car, driving recklessly, taking it out late at night and accelerating through the darkness into the tight turns of the winding roads around the Manse.

We'd been stuck in unmoving traffic on a straight stretch of Route 1 in New Jersey when she first told me this. Even then I could feel her antagonism as she handled the car. I was never again entirely comfortable when she was behind the wheel, and that much was unchanged as she drove us from the station.

"You left in a hurry," I said.

I hadn't realized until then how angry I was at her for closing that cab door and disappearing so abruptly, and how scared I was that she might disappear again.

"Something occurred to me, and I had to work it out."

"You could have worked it out in New York," I said. "I would have loaned you pen and paper."

"That's not really my medium anymore, as you know."

When I didn't say anything she added, "It felt too nice

being with you. If I hadn't left, then I might have stayed forever."

"That wouldn't have been so bad," I said.

"But I knew I had to leave. There was something I needed to do."

The Old Manse was about ten miles from town. It sat on a quiet road amid a long row of horse farms with tall, white fences and empty, green fields broken up by the occasional animal. I hadn't been to the house in years, but everything looked the same. It was a white-shingled New England colonial with a large front porch, set on a smaller plot of land than its neighbors, but with a pool in the backyard and not far from it a small work shed that had been Sophie's father's home office.

It was an oddly warm day, more like summer than early autumn, and the afternoon sun throbbed in an otherwise empty sky. Sophie showed me to the guest room, where I set my bag down unopened on the bed.

"Do you want to go for a swim?" she asked. "It might be the last chance of the season."

"I didn't bring a suit."

"You can take one from my dad."

We went upstairs, down the long hall to her parents' room, which had never changed in all my visits. There was a blown-up photograph of Sophie at two or three years old framed on one wall and a photograph of the family together on the wall facing it. Sophie found a pair of her father's trunks in the chest beside the bed and left me to change. The suit was short, with blue and white horizontal stripes. It was big around the waist, but I pulled the drawstring tight. I brought my clothes back to the room downstairs, where I quickly unpacked before heading outside.

Sophie wasn't out by the pool, but a pile of clean towels waited on a wrought-iron table between two Adirondack chairs on the deck. In the middle of the wall at the pool's shallow end, an underwater light made the surface shimmer as though reflecting the sun. I stood at the opposite end, looking down at the light. Then I dove in.

As soon as I passed into the cold water, I felt the swimsuit give way, slipping off my hips and down my legs. Rather than reach for it, I freed my feet with a scissor kick and swam toward the bottom, touching a hand against the pool's dark tiles. I went on to the wall in front of me, to the light, following the upward slope as it shallowed. My lungs were empty before I was halfway across. The pain came first to my chest and then extended up to my neck, calling me to the surface for a breath. Another, stronger force kept me down, sending me to the light. I swam with quick, thrusting strokes and violent kicks, my movements graceless and desperate. Everything depended on going on. All at once the end of the pool jumped out at me, and I nearly crashed against the light. I pressed my hands forward as though breaking a fall and thrust myself up to the air, which only a moment earlier had seemed so far away.

"Quite a performance," Sophie said while I gasped angrily. She stood on the deck in a light blue robe, with a cigarette in her hand. She took a drag as she circled the pool to the deep end, near the place where I had stood before diving in. When she got there, she dropped the cigarette, which crackled as it went out on the wet deck. She took off her robe to reveal no suit underneath. She stood for a moment before me. Then she was in the water.

I first saw Sophie naked a few days after Max's visit to New Hampton. She and I had spent the night drinking in her room and talking about books. This wasn't yet our regular habit, and it was unclear to me how the night would end. Eventually I fell asleep on her couch. When I woke she stood topless, changing for bed. Her dark, teardrop breasts hung loose from her body as she leaned over an open dresser drawer. She found a black T-shirt and put it on.

When she reached for the button of her jeans, I considered letting her know that I was awake, but I didn't make a sound. She shook teasingly as she slipped her pants over her hips. With both thumbs in the elastic waistband of her white cotton underwear, she pulled them down her legs in a single fluid motion. She gave a little jump when she reached her feet. Her legs splayed out in landing, and a few stray dark hairs peeked out between them.

She turned. Her T-shirt had Mickey Mouse on its front, and her hair below matched the black shirt so closely that they seemed to be of a piece. She didn't look embarrassed or surprised to find me watching her.

"Go back to sleep, you perv," she said.

I rolled over on the couch, turning away from her. In another moment, the light went out. Even in the darkness I shut my eyes, like a child counting in a game of hide and seek. In fact, I did count quietly, holding my breath. Just as I reached zero she lay down beside me. She set her head between my shoulder blades. In a few minutes her breathing fell into a slow and regular rhythm, with the lightest hint of a snore on its exhale, and I knew she was asleep.

When I woke, she sat in her armchair in the corner, wearing the same black Mickey Mouse T-shirt with a pair of blue and white striped pajama bottoms, reading a Thomas Bernhard novel—*Gargoyles*, I think it was, or maybe *The Loser*. She smiled at me as I sat up on the couch. Another month passed before we wound up in bed together.

Now she moved quickly through the pool, though from where I was watching she appeared to do nothing to propel herself, like a bird that stays perfectly still while cutting through the sky. She seemed not so much a body as a shimmering trick of water and light. As she neared the wall I stepped aside, waiting for her to come up. Instead she executed a perfect flip turn, pushing her feet against the wall and shooting back from where she'd come. I felt suffocated, watching her swim away and remembering my own pounding chest. I wanted to pull her to the surface. I had to remind myself that she wasn't going to drown. If she needed air, she would come up for it.

Nonetheless, I felt relieved when she reached the other end. Even then she didn't emerge right away. She dropped to the bottom of the pool, curled in a ball like a sinking rock. When she hit the bottom, she unloaded the spring of herself, pressing her feet against the tile and sending herself upward.

In another moment she was back on the deck, hunched over with her hands on her knees, catching her breath. She picked up her robe and pulled it back on. The whole thing had taken only a minute. She looked down at the pool defiantly, even a bit angrily, as if I had told her she couldn't do it and now she had proven me wrong. Her breath steadied and she reached into the pocket of her robe for her cigarettes. By the time she got one lit she'd circled the deck and settled in a chair.

I swam to retrieve my suit, pulled it on, and climbed out of the pool. There was a second robe among the towels, and I put it on before sitting down next to her.

"My father and I built this together," she said, waving as if she might be talking about the yard, the house, the whole world around us.

"Built what?" I asked.

"This," she said. She pounded a foot against the wooden deck beneath us. "It took a few weeks in the summer after the pool was put in. He romanticized physical labor, like Tolstoy with his threshing. Every summer weekend he spent shirtless out in the sun, landscaping or gardening. And he always wanted me to help. We built that shack over there, where he set up his little home office. But that year it was the deck. He circled the pool with his posthole digger, shoving it into the ground, twisting it in the earth to cut away roots, then pulling them out and tossing them aside. I followed, planting a post in each hole and pouring quick-set concrete from a big bag I dragged along from hole to hole."

"Seems pretty sturdy," I said, and I gave the boards a playful kick. She didn't smile.

"My grandfather was a mason in central Pennsylvania." She'd told me all this before, but I didn't interrupt. "All through high school and college my father spent his summers outside, carrying stones. For the rest of his life I think he believed there was something insufficient about office work. Real labor was something done with your hands. I think he considered it a failing that his occupation didn't yield tangible products. It earned him lots of money with which tangible products could be bought, but that's not the same thing. Mostly, he was disappointed that he couldn't pass on a trade to me. Three generations of Wilder masons. Not so long, he'd admit, in the stream of time, but something. That line of three had ended with his father. As far as he was concerned, shared work was the authentic basis for a father's relationship with his child. It was an apprenticeship. A trade was passed along, and it could only be passed along in the doing of it. So the work had two products. You have a deck, and then you have the knowledge transmitted in making it."

"It's nice to have those memories," I said.

"I hated it," Sophie answered. "It was playacting. He was a banker. Building decks wasn't his real job, and it wasn't ever going to be mine. What kind of kid wants to spend her summer break doing manual labor in the sun? I wanted to sit inside and read. Now, I wish I had some practical skills besides pouring concrete and dragging the hose around the yard. Maybe I'd have something to do with the rest of my life."

"Writing is a practical skill," I said. "You wind up with a product at the end."

"Something else I realized," she said. "My old preference for the self-contained work of art, which I'd always taken to be a cold aesthetic principle, was really just a sentimental predilection for craftsmanship. I'm my father's child after all."

"So where's the problem in that?"

"The problem is I don't know what that craftsmanship is supposed to be for. What have you got when you're done? You can't sit on it, no matter how sturdy it is."

"But you've made something beautiful."

She let out a long stream of smoke and then waved at it, mixing it into the air in front of her.

"I'm not sure that's possible."

"Since when?"

"Beauty comes from the fair and fit, Augustine says."

"I don't follow."

"In other words, it's a kind of byproduct of the elegance with which an object meets its purpose. A work whose purpose is to be beautiful gets trapped in circularity. It can't ever succeed in that goal. Beauty can only be arrived at while meeting some real need. So what's the point? What's the thing writing is supposed to do, the aim it's after that along the way produces its beauty?"

"You don't think the need for beauty is a real need?"

"Sure we need it," she said. "But it already exists without us. 'Two things fill the mind with ever new and increasing wonder and awe. The starry heavens above me and the moral law within me.'"

"You've stumped me," I said.

"It's Kant."

"You've been reading Kant?"

"Bill Crane told me that."

I wasn't ready for him yet. I wanted a chance to be with Sophie without the man's presence between us.

"Why did you invite me here?" I asked.

"Because I wanted to see you again, and not at that house with Max and all his friends. And because I wanted to say good-bye."

"You came back to say good-bye?"

"I'm going away."

"You were already away."

"Now I'm going for good. It's time for me to be ushered off the stage."

"I'm not going to usher you off," I said. "I want to be with you. I want to marry you."

It was true.

"That's impossible, Charlie. I'm already married."

"You're divorced."

"I'm separated."

"So when does your divorce go through? I can wait."

"It doesn't go through, Charlie. There is no divorce. I was married in the Church. That means I stay married."

"Does Tom feel that way?"

"It doesn't matter how Tom feels. It's not up to him."

"So if he goes off and marries that girl we saw in the street, you'll still be his wife as far as you're concerned?"

"That's right."

"What about annulments? I mean, you were young when you got married, and you didn't stay together that long. Couldn't you get a priest to do something?"

"You're missing the point. I knew the vow I was taking. What would be the grounds for an annulment?"

"You can make something up. People do it."

"Granted, people do it. I'm not going to."

"It's irrational, Sophie. This isn't 1940. And it doesn't have anything to do with the things that religion is supposed to be about—charity, and love, and being good to others. Punishing yourself doesn't achieve anything."

"You're right about that much," she said.

"So you're going to be alone for the rest of your life, because you made a mistake when you were twenty-two?"

"If my husband doesn't come back, I will."

"God couldn't possibly want you to suffer for the rest of your life when you didn't do anything wrong."

"You may be right about that, too. I can't know what God wants. I only know what I promised."

"Tom broke the promise, not you."

"My promise wasn't to him."

"It's over, Sophie. You kept your end of the bargain. It's not your fault."

"This isn't about whose fault it is."

"It doesn't make sense," I said.

"I never said it made sense. I don't even understand it myself, but I'm not going to change my mind."

"How can you be sure?"

"Because," she said, "I do not hope to turn again."

Pushing further with the conversation meant ruining what

was left of our night. I told myself that I could convince her before my stay was over.

"Let's go inside," Sophie said. "I'll get dinner ready."

In the kitchen, she poured us each a glass of wine.

"So you're really going away?" I asked her.

"I am," she said.

"Where are you going?"

"I haven't entirely figured that out yet. I just know it's time for me to leave this place."

She took a tray of baked pasta from the oven and served us each a bowl. I followed her to the table.

"How long will you be gone?" I asked, as we sat down at the table. "You don't really mean for good."

"I'm not sure about that, either. In the meantime, you should stay here as long as you want. My father's old work shed makes a nice writing space."

"It's a kind offer, Sophie, but I couldn't do that."

"You should stay," she said. "That is, I want you to. I'm not just being polite."

"I appreciate it, but I really don't think I could stay without you here."

"Suit yourself," she told me. "But think about it before you decide. I'm leaving it entirely to you."

Sophie poured herself another glass of wine.

"What I said before, about hating working with my father?"

"Yes?"

"It wasn't just that," Sophie said. "Most of the time I hated him. He was such an unhappy man. I think he liked working that way because he thought that if he exhausted himself his mind would quiet down a little bit. I think his brain was torturing him. All of this, of course, I decided later.

At the time I just thought he was unpleasant to be around. Maybe he'd done something he really regretted. Maybe he just wanted to forget. I wish I'd been more understanding."

I hadn't seen her crying since the day that she told me she was pregnant. She might have made the same connection, because she said, "I thought about him after the miscarriage. I still don't why."

She had never told me before how the pregnancy ended. I didn't know what to say.

"Enough of all that," Sophie said, wiping the tears that had now made their way to her cheeks. "I don't want to spoil our meal."

After my own father died, we'd driven in a long procession to the family plot on Long Island, where we buried him beside his own father. Before that, there had been a funeral mass, where the priest said that my father had been baptized into Christ and now had died into eternal life. Though the first part was strictly true—he'd been baptized a Catholic— I can't speak to the rest. He wasn't a particularly religious man. That is to say, it wasn't the first thing someone would say about him, so it seemed strange that it should be the last, that we should memorialize him in this way.

My uncle had taken care of all the arrangements, and he had a strong sense of tradition, of what was proper for the family. Whatever your beliefs on every other day of your life, my uncle said, marriage and death were the times to return to the Church. My grandmother wanted to see her son laid to rest beside her husband, near the place where she would soon go, which couldn't happen without a proper burial. I didn't care about any of this at the time. What difference did it make to my dead father? Such things were done for the survivors. But now I thought differently.

There were still people like Sophie, who took the words of faith as more than words. In light of that fact, it seemed wrong that all these others spoke for appearance's sake.

This was what I thought as I followed Sophie down the hall back to my room that night. We had finished two bottles of wine by then, having moved from the kitchen table to the den, where we'd sat beside each other on the couch. Now we arrived at the door to my room and stood uncomfortably near each other for a moment. Then I pulled her close, and she put her arms around me.

"I love you, Sophie," I told her.

"I love you too," she said.

She pushed the door open and led me inside. I didn't know what to make of this after what she'd told me at dinner about her marriage, but I followed her to the bed. I had imagined, over the years, being with Sophie again, though I knew how unlikely it was. Now we were both nervous and awkward and a little drunk. It took some time for us to find the rhythm of each other's bodies. She pulled me on top of her, guided me inside, and then thrashed as if in fear, as if protecting herself. But when I gave way, she pulled me closer again. Almost as soon as we'd finished, she was up from the bed.

"Goodnight, Charlie," she said.

"Do you really have to leave?"

"Yes," she said.

"I wish things could be different."

She leaned over the bed to kiss me.

"Then write it different."

3

SOPHIE DIDN'T SLEEP well that night. She felt strange out of her own bed, in no bed at all, with one stiff drink in her belly and a second swirling in her head. She woke several times and sat up in darkness, listening to the hum of the world and wondering if she had energy left to make another life for herself. At last enough light came through the blinds to allow for giving up on the night.

She pulled on her jeans and went to the kitchen, where she fried two eggs and put on a pot of coffee. Later she would make something for Crane, something he wouldn't eat, but now she would let him sleep as long as he could. That would be hours, probably—it was just after 6:00 AM. Once he was awake, she would bring him a bowl of nuts and another protein drink, and their first full day together would begin. In the meantime, he was safe in bed, and there was nothing she could do for him by standing in the kitchen. After she finished eating, she went looking for a church.

An old man slept on the sidewalk outside the building, tucked into a tunnel of cardboard, his feet wrapped in newspaper. Sophie walked around him to the corner. The streets were nearly empty, and the morning light gave the air a poignant clarity.

It didn't take long to find a Catholic church on a side street off Tompkins Square. The block was being developed, with three high-rise apartment buildings nearing completion. These unfinished hulks were already taller than the church, which would once have been the highest point on that street, visible from a distance, as churches had once been the highest points in every neighborhood, in every town. As it was, Sophie was nearly in front of it before she found it. A sign outside announced a daily mass at 7:00 AM.

The church looked bigger inside than it had from the street, and the lights above bathed the tiled floor between irregular spiderwebs of shadow. Four old women filled the first row, but otherwise the pews were empty. Sophie entered quietly and knelt to pray. She had always prayed first for Tom, and it felt inconstant to do otherwise now.

If he returned, she would take him in—he was still her husband—but knowing this wasn't the same thing as wanting him back. She tried to imagine the other girl, not out of real interest but because she thought she should. She found that it wasn't easy to take an interest in people. It brought responsibility. This was God's work, Sophie thought: to think of us all the time, to continue imagining us, so that we might continue to exist.

She prayed next for Tom's sibling, the sister whose existence she now imagined. Doing so brought to mind naturally enough her own unborn child, whom she considered with a sad curiosity. It seemed likely to be the last child she would have. There weren't as many chances as one might have thought to make a life.

A bell rang in the sacristy, and the priest appeared with a single acolyte, a young girl of ten or eleven, carrying the cross. The first words of the mass disoriented Sophie. It took a moment for the feeling to resolve itself. There had been no indication of a foreign-language mass on the schedule outside, but the neighborhood was mostly Hispanic, or had been until the luxury buildings started going up, so it shouldn't have surprised Sophie to hear the priest's greeting made in Spanish. She didn't know the language, but she knew the ceremony, so it was easy to follow along. Countless generations had spent their lives going to masses said in a language they didn't speak out in the world, no longer a public language at all but the private means by which God communicated to his followers. The combination of familiarity and strangeness returned Sophie for the first time in years to the shocked grace she'd felt on that day when everything had changed. It arrived occasionally like this, unbidden, but the moment she recognized its presence it was gone, leaving her to ache in its absence. She wanted to think that returning to this mass on another morning would bring it back, but she knew it would not. It couldn't be found by looking. You could only wait for it.

At the kiss of peace, the priest stepped down from the altar and gave each of the women in the front row a lingering hug as though they were family, which they well might have been. He walked back to Sophie's pew, and she slid toward the center aisle, preparing to offer her hand. But he took her into his arms just as he had the others and said, speaking in English as if he'd known all along that she'd wandered in by mistake, "Peace be with you."

Back in the apartment, Sophie felt a new reserve of energy available to her. It was after eight o'clock, and she decided to look in on Crane. The hospice worker wouldn't arrive for three more hours, so she had plenty of time to get him up and make him presentable. She wasn't sure why she should feel this necessary, why she needed whoever was sent to believe that she was taking proper care of him. She poured a glass of the drink and brought it to the bedroom. She knocked lightly on his door. When no answer came, she let herself in.

The first thing she noticed was the empty bed. She stood in the doorway puzzling over the sight until her attention turned to where he lay on the floor. He was so still, his position so awkward, that she was certain at the sight of him that he was dead. She knelt to find him not only breathing but also awake, his open eyes staring up at her in terror and shame.

"Are you all right?" she asked.

He made some effort to answer, but no sounds came. She reached her arms around his chest to pull him up into a sitting position. As she did, she nearly recoiled at the smell, like an open wound left untended.

Sitting up, he came back to himself a bit.

"I fell out of bed."

"When did it happen?"

He looked up at her helplessly. What means did he have for marking the passing time?

"I called out for you, but then I got tired."

"From now on," she said, "I'll sleep in here, so I'll know if it happens again."

She handed him the glass and he took a careful sip. While he drank, she turned on the lights in the room and opened a window to let out the smell. She sat down beside him. When he had finished the glass, she tried to stand him up. It seemed impossible that he could have weakened so much overnight.

"I can't get up now," he said.

He was calmer, and his eyes had lost their look of empty fear. She thought of his struggling in the night, perhaps for hours, before giving up, exhausted but too frightened to sleep.

"When you're ready," she said, "we'll get you back into bed and you can get some rest. I'll give you another pill."

"I don't want to get in bed."

"We'll move you into the middle," she said. "I'll stay right here and make sure you don't fall out."

"It's not that."

He had something more to say, but he couldn't bring himself to say it.

"What is it?"

"I shit myself," he told her. "I don't want to bring it into my bed."

"We'll get you cleaned up."

She gathered what she would need to wash him there on the floor. From the bathroom she took some towels and a bar of soap. She found a bucket beneath the sink in the kitchen and filled it with warm water before bringing it back beside the bed along with a sponge and a roll of paper towels. She sat down and pulled off Crane's sweaty shirt. It clung thickly to his body in resistance, and when it came off it brought a thin layer of skin with it. It wasn't just the part of him covered in burns but all of his skin that seemed enflamed.

Sophie soaped the water and dipped the sponge—a kitchen sponge, probably harsh against him, but all she could find. She squeezed it and ran it slowly down the outside of his left arm. He winced as she lifted the arm and ran the sponge back up the inner part. When she reached his armpit, she found the skin festering. She had torn some of it off while raising his arm, and a small wound had opened. He flinched when the sponge passed over it. She wasn't sure this was good for the wound, but she didn't know what else to do. When she'd finished she dried off his arm and let it rest back at his side. She went to the other one and from there to his chest and his back, after which there was nothing left but to pull off his soiled boxer shorts. They left a trail of greenish brown along his legs as they came off. Sophie dropped them into the trash bin near the bed.

She couldn't keep herself from taking a moment to look him over. His belly fell over his gray-black pubic hair, visible only in odd, isolated patches, like weeds growing through cracks in concrete. Below that was an inert jumble of skin, one part nearly indistinguishable from another. It was mostly tucked away between his legs as though in hiding, with the reddish flap of foreskin pinched against his thigh. The sponge felt suddenly heavy in her hands, and she let it fall back into the bucket. When she pulled his legs apart, she saw that she couldn't go about the rest of the job from the front, couldn't watch him mutely watching her work. She moved him onto his side and approached from behind, using the paper towel to wipe him. What she found between his legs was the same color'and consistency as the drink she'd been forcing on him. She put a towel down on the floor and rolled him onto it.

When she'd cleaned up the floor and dressed him, Crane agreed to get back into bed. He was stronger now, or perhaps just more willing to help. They got him up from the floor without trouble and moved him to the center of the mattress. Sophie set pillows along his sides to keep him from rolling. She gave him a sleeping pill and retreated to a chair at the other end of the room, where she sat listening to him breathe.

Crane was still asleep, and Sophie still sitting, when the buzzer sounded. A round, severe-looking woman stood on the landing with what looked like a large gym bag slung over her shoulder. She had dark black hair pulled into a ponytail.

"I'm Sarah," she said. "The hospice sent me."

Sophie introduced herself, offering a hand that the woman didn't take.

"Where's your father?" Sarah asked.

"He's sleeping. He had a rough night."

"Has the doctor prescribed something for that?"

"Yes, but he fell out of bed."

The woman nodded. Her interest in the problem seemed mostly academic.

"We'll send over something that you can set up to keep that from happening again."

"That would be a relief," Sophie said.

Sarah took a seat on the couch and emptied her bag while she explained the services the hospice would provide. Insurance would pay for someone to come to the apartment for an hour each day.

"If you need more time than that," she said, "you can bring him in to us. He'll get all the attention he needs."

"He wants to stay at home."

"Is it just you taking care of him?"

"Yes."

"It's going to be quite a challenge, I'd imagine." There was no reproach, merely a statement of professional opinion. When Sophie didn't respond she went on. "I'll look in on him now. You're welcome to step out for a bit if you have errands to run. I can stay a little longer, this once, since I'm sure you've got some catching up to do."

Earlier that morning, this hour would not have felt so precious, but now Sophie knew that she could no longer leave Crane alone. She would have to make the most of her time outside. If she hurried, she could get uptown and back without making Sarah wait too long. If her job would consist mainly in sitting up while Crane slept, she would need more books, though she no longer had any illusions about reading them to him.

She didn't have to worry about running into Tom at the apartment, since he'd already abandoned it for whatever fashionable corner of Brooklyn or the West Village the girl had made her home for the summer. The doorman greeted Sophie as warmly as always. She wondered if he knew that Tom had moved out.

Letting herself into the apartment, Sophie felt as though she'd been away a long time. On the shelf near her desk, she found another book by Thomas Merton, *The Waters of Siloe*, about life at Gethsemane, the Trappist monastery in Kentucky where he had lived and written. Sophie had always felt envious, when reading it, that Merton's conversion had brought him to silence and solitude. At the time it had seemed natural that her own had chased her into the sacrament of marriage, into sharing her life with another. It seemed now that it had never needed to be that way.

A few miles from her parents' house in Connecticut was an abbey of Benedictine nuns. She had driven by it many times while growing up and after her conversion she had made a few visits there. It was the most peaceful place she'd ever been. It had not occurred to her until it was too late that she might choose that kind of peace. She didn't know how the women there lived, but she imagined it wasn't so different from Merton's Trappist existence. Perhaps that's what she had been called to all along, without knowing it: contemplation. Would she have the courage for it, if it came to that? She couldn't afford to be wrong another time. She couldn't keep going from life to life.

It took an active effort to stop pursuing this line of thought. She needed to get herself back to Crane. She put a few other books in her bag and looked around to see what else she should take along. Her notebook still sat where Tom had set it down on the night he left. If she took it now, it wouldn't be to work on the grant whose deadline was just a week away. She would be using it to write about Crane.

Before leaving, she called the director of the speech clinic. She got the woman's voice mail, and so it was painless enough to explain that her father was very ill—dying, in fact, she didn't hesitate to say—which would prevent her from finishing the proposal in time. Of course, she would not bill the clinic for the hours she had already put in, and she would be back as soon as possible to find another appropriate funding source for them. She hung up and gave a last look around before leaving. There was nothing else she needed there.

The lobby mailbox was full, as if Sophie had been gone for weeks instead of just overnight. A single large envelope took up most of the space, the rest being a normal day's worth of junk. The envelope was addressed to her, from Peters and Ryan, the agency where Greg worked. It was oppressive even to think of him. She considered throwing the package out, but she slipped it instead into her bag.

"I put a pad underneath him on the bed, in case there's another accident," Sarah said by way of greeting when Sophie returned. She gave no indication of how she knew about the first accident. "You'll want to buy some diapers, though."

Sophie thanked her and walked her to the door.

"They'll send someone else over tomorrow," Sarah continued as Sophie let her out. "My day off. But I'll see you again in a few days."

Alone again, Sophie returned to the bedroom, where Crane was still asleep. It was early afternoon, and she was exhausted. If he slept all day, he would be up through the night, and she would stay up with him. She thought she should try to sleep while she could. Instead she brought her bag to the chair in the corner and took out Greg's package. There was a book inside, with a handwritten note paper-clipped to it: *Here's the novel I mentioned on the phone. Maybe consider working on something in this vein? Of course it's up to you. The old man idea could still work.*

The book's cover had a photograph of a young man and woman walking away from each other on a snow-covered street. Between them was the title, *In the City of My Birth*. At the bottom of the picture, along the sidewalk's edge, was the author's name: Charles R. Blakeman.

Charlie had sent an advance copy to Sophie months earlier, and she'd started reading it several times, but she couldn't get out of the first chapter. It told the story of a boy like Charlie, living with a boy like Max, going to literary parties, taking drugs, sleeping with pretty young publicists. It was all so sad to Sophie, and she couldn't tell if Charlie had meant it to be.

He was writing about a world she didn't share with him, but this shouldn't have been enough to put her off. Was it that part of her had wanted, after all, to live in that world with him? Did she wish that she'd spent the years since parting with Charlie in some other way? He had meant so much to her once, and they had both had such promise. Perhaps the sadness came from knowing that this book—her own slim book already forgotten—was all this promise had amounted to. For it seemed to her that there would be no follow-ups.

She could have married him if she'd wanted, though it probably wouldn't have turned out any better than the marriage she'd had. Tom had led her to the Church, and no matter how things ended between them, she didn't wish that she'd been led otherwise. But if she didn't regret the life she'd given up, why did she find it so hard just to read Charlie's book?

Something strong had kept her from it, something she couldn't understand. She wanted better for him, wanted better for both of them. After a while she couldn't even look at the plain black and white cover of the advance copy. It shamed her. One day she threw it out impulsively, and she'd been trying to forget about it ever since. She knew she should have called to congratulate him when the book came out. But that would have meant admitting that she hadn't read it, for he would certainly ask her what she'd thought, and she couldn't lie to Charlie, at least not about that. So she'd done nothing at all.

There had been a time when she thought of Charlie, like her writing, as something precious she needed to give up as proof of her faith. It didn't make sense, she knew, but the feeling was unmistakable. Looking at the book's cover, she remembered how it had seemed to them that their lives were intertwined irrevocably no matter what else happened, like the paths of two characters in a novel. She still felt this way, the difference being that she knew now who the author of her story was. But why send her this book? Why send her back to Charlie, or Charlie back to her?

"What is it?"

Across the room Bill Crane sat upright in bed, looking at her. She'd nearly forgotten that he was there. With one hand she waved the book vaguely at him while wiping her tears with the other.

"Just something I'm reading."

"You're not reading, you're just looking at the cover and crying."

His voice no longer had a full range of tones to it; everything came out uncertainly, so she couldn't tell if he meant to be cruel.

"I used to know the author."

"An old flame?" he asked in the same flat voice.

"Something like that," she said. Despite herself she added, "I was in love with him."

"Did Tom know?"

"This was all before Tom."

"I see," he said. "My son was the consolation prize."

"No, it wasn't that." She decided that if she was going to tell him anything, she shouldn't spare herself. "I fucked his cousin."

"The temptations of the flesh."

"It was the only thing I could think to do that he would never forgive."

She cried more openly now, unembarrassed in front of this man whom she had washed and changed like an infant that morning.

"Still hung up on him, though, after all these years?"

"I was thinking of something else," she said. "I got pregnant."

She had never told this to anyone who didn't have a stake in the story, never told it just for the telling.

"You have a kid?"

"I lost it."

"Let me guess: that's when you found God."

"Just about."

"You're more predictable than I thought."

He seemed to know that the worst thing he could do was reduce her faith to a banality.

"I don't know how much the two had to do with each other."

"So the little guy's in limbo now? Is that how it works?"

It was an effort not to rise to his provocations, even though she recognized them for what they were and he sat helpless in bed.

"No," she said. "That's not how it works. Unbaptized infants are entrusted to the mercy of God." How many times had she said these words to herself? "But God has not revealed to the Church their ultimate fate."

"In plain English, then, you don't know if your child is in hell?"

"That's right."

"But you worship a God that might have put it there?"

"Where do you think your child is?" she asked, knowing as she said it that she was making a terrible mistake.

"Where do I think Tom is?"

"Not Tom," she said. "The other one."

His eyes opened wide and he took a sharp breath. Then he went into a kind of fit, letting out a wheezing sound. She was killing him. But as she approached she saw that he was laughing.

"We have something in common, then" he said. "We both left children in the flames."

"You really are a monster."

"Of course I am. You must have known that long before we met."

"It doesn't make any difference that I'm taking care of you?"

"Sure it does," he said. "I hate you for it."

She stopped halfway between chair and bed.

"I'm only trying to keep you from suffering. I could have left you there on the floor in your own shit. Would that have been better?"

"The suffering would all be over now if you hadn't sent that woman to check on me."

This was undeniably so. But what could she do about it now? Let him starve to death? Let him spend his last days in pain?

"You're not going to chase me away," she said. "Nothing you say, no matter how awful, is going to make me leave you here to rot."

But chase her away he did, at least as far as the living room, to which she retreated after giving him a pill. She couldn't believe that he'd joked about his dead child, even to punish her. His callousness made her think that he'd set the fire on purpose, that Tom's very worst ideas about the man were true, though she couldn't say why. There was a long way between making a joke about such a thing and actually doing it.

She'd brought Charlie's book out of the room with her, but she set it down and fished under the couch for the folder. She flipped through the clippings she'd already read, and then through several more that merely recapped the same information. Then she reached the first to mention a suspicion of arson. It said only that police were investigating the conditions under which the fire began. It also made brief mention of Crane's condition, still critical, but it drew no connection between him and the unsettled question. By this time, the story had moved to the farther reaches of the paper, but the next story was back on the front page, with a headline that ran across three columns:

"In Deadly Blaze, Police Suspicion Lands on Victims' Child."

The article began, "Police are investigating the possibility that a house fire that killed a pregnant Columbia woman and left her husband, a Missouri professor, in critical condition was started by the couple's eight-year-old son."

Sophie read no further. She shut the folder violently, as if to thrust the very idea out of her head. She wanted no part of this new knowledge. It was a false lead, she knew. Crane had started the fire. The fact that the police hadn't realized it right away meant nothing. But this new possibility, once planted, was difficult to dislodge. It explained why Tom had never wanted to talk about his father, why he'd placed the topic permanently off limits. If he had done it, it would have been an accident, a horrible thing to have lived with all this time.

If she could have returned to the wondering ignorance in which Tom had tried to keep her, she would. She got up from the couch, wishing she could walk away from all these possibilities. Back in the bedroom, Bill was asleep. She shut the light and sat down in the corner. When she'd left the room a few minutes before, she'd been exhausted. Now she was entirely awake. She reached out for her bag on the floor. It was too dark to read, but even turning pages might calm her. She didn't go to the bag expecting to hear that click, like loose change, but that is what she found. She heard it again as her hand hit upon the plastic bottle.

These sleeping pills were prescribed for everyday insomnia, not just for terminal patients. She could have gotten her own just by asking. There was no harm in taking one, if only to keep to Crane's schedule. Otherwise, she might never sleep.

4

WALKING DOWNSTAIRS THE next morning, I worried that the creaking of the narrow wooden steps might wake Sophie. After each one I stopped while the floorboards settled, and I felt the house beneath my feet. I ducked into the dining room. A single speeding car came and went outside. The sound of it lingered well after it was gone. Everything went still, and I went still with it.

I put on a pot of coffee in the kitchen and thought about Sophie's invitation to stay. I was sure that her offer was serious, but that also meant she was serious about leaving. I tried to imagine a future at the Manse, but I couldn't imagine one without her. I decided to make breakfast, as if this domestic act might help her imagine our life together and make her want to stay. The refrigerator held only a stick of butter, a withered head of lettuce, and an old pint of milk. The freezer was in a similar state, with a single empty ice-cube tray and an uninviting mound of plastic-wrapped meat. If I was going to take care of Sophie, I would have to start by shopping.

Outside, the sun sat low between two hills in the distance, still sharing the sky with a pale half-moon. The clock on the Jaguar's dashboard read 6:02 AM. In New York I could sleep until noon and still be tired, but that morning I felt refreshed, as though the perpetual fatigue of the city was a kind of spiritual exhaustion from which I was beginning to recover. Whatever I needed to make breakfast could be picked up on a short trip to town, and I'd have the food waiting when Sophie woke up. While we sat eating on the porch, I would explain the solution that was only then coming to me. She could be married to Tom forever, and I wouldn't interfere with that, but we would be together. Despite what had happened the night before, we didn't need to sleep together. But we needed to share our lives. I would get her to admit that much over breakfast.

Strictly speaking, I knew how to drive—I was licensed to do it after taking driver's ed at St. Albert's—but I'd never owned a car. The last time I'd driven had been in that Jaguar, with Sophie in the passenger seat. She'd let me take the wheel on a trip to the multiplex near school. I'd nearly crashed along the way. After the movie she took the keys and drove us back to campus. "If we're going to get killed," she'd said, "I'm the one who's going to do it."

I pulled slowly out of the driveway, signaling my turn though there was no other car in sight. I followed the curve of the road, concentrating on keeping the wheel steady. The feel of the car came back to me as I guided it through the turn. When the road straightened for a stretch, I put on the radio and rolled the window down. I stuck my arm out in the wind as I picked up speed.

We'd passed through town on our way from the station, so it should have been easy to find my way back. But I missed a turn somewhere. After a few miles the road became unfamiliar. I was sure that Main Street was some-where to my right, so I took the next turn in that direction. But the road twisted, sending me in the same direction I'd already been going, away from both town and the Manse. It ran one way, so I could only go on wherever it was taking me. There was no one around at that hour to ask for direc-tions. There weren't even houses on the side of the road, only fields where horses paced and ate. The road turned uphill, tracing a series of cutbacks that I followed help-lessly. As that helplessness settled, I spotted a little wooden sign near a dirt path that split off from the road: The Ab-bey of Regina Laudis.

I'd known the place existed, that it was a few miles from the Manse. Sophie had mentioned it to me, long be-fore her conversion, as a local curiosity. But stumbling on it now meant something. I don't know what I expected to find at the end of that dirt path, but I came upon a half-filled parking lot. Beside it stood a building in the straight-lined style of postwar suburban churches, similar to the one my grandparents had attended each Sunday on Long Island, the one to which I'd gone for my father's funeral. I followed a small group of people inside. Everyone who entered found a pew and knelt in silence. Reflexively, I did the same.

For twelve years, I had knelt that way each morning in the St. Albert's chapel. Sometime around fifth grade, I'd stopped trying to pray during those minutes of silence be-fore our daily chapel talk began. Instead I thought about the day ahead of me, or the homework I hadn't done the night before. Once this became unbearable, I would give up those thoughts and just turn words around in my head until we stood to sing from our thick red hymnals. Sometimes a sentence would click—not the meaning of it exactly, but its shape—and I would try desperately to hold on to it until I got to class, where I could write it down. On the page it usually sat lifeless, making me wonder what had excited me about it. The words retained their power perhaps a dozen times over a span of years, and the resulting satisfaction lasted through the day. I'd forgotten this fact until that morning: my first real efforts at writing had happened while I was on my knees.

A bell rang and a line of nuns entered from the sacristy. An ornate metal fence, reaching nearly to the ceiling, separated them from the congregation as they surrounded the altar. No doubt the barrier had some theological justification, perhaps as protection from us sinners outside, but it seemed that the wall might as easily serve to keep them in as to keep us out. It hinted that these women weren't contained quite of their own volition, that the sight of us among them might drive the weaker-willed to escape.

There were about thirty nuns, some old and infirm, most in late middle age. The occasional woman even as young as my mother surprised me. But the last to enter was no older than I was. The hushed church seemed to fall into a deeper silence with her appearance, though most of the congregation must have been used to the sight. The shock didn't come entirely from her youth, but also from her beauty. She would have been beautiful in any setting, but in this place her beauty seemed like a beatitude granted to the rest of us. What could have led her to this place?

Some prejudice on my part, or failure of imagination, gave a sinister turn to every answer I considered. No one retreated so completely from the world unless there was something unbearable about it. There had been abuse by a father or a boyfriend. There had been an assault, an unwanted pregnancy, some kind of scandal for which she was now making amends. I knew this last notion was anti-quated—not just the idea of the religious life as sanctuary, but the idea of sanctuary itself, of escape from the shame of the past. The past could now simply be forgotten. It was no longer possible to disgrace oneself. If any of the women in front of me had come to the abbey to redeem a wayward youth, it would have been one of the stooped nonagenar-ians, children of the Depression, old enough to have lived in a world where certain mistakes were irrevocable.

The women took up places beside the altar and started to sing. To chant, I should say. I remembered a time in college when Gregorian chant had been common back-ground music for dorm room study. It was soothing, even inspiring, but it was also popular as an ironic statement on our artificial surroundings. We sat in medieval turrets, in monastic solitude, reading some gloss on Derrida. What I witnessed at the abbey that morning was entirely different. It was happening right in front of me, emanating not from weak computer speakers but from the other side of that metal divide. There wasn't a hint of irony to it, no sense of an outdated habit being cultivated or an endangered art preserved. They sang as though it was simply the best way they knew of being in the world. And the people around me listened as though listening was their own best way.

When the chant was done, two priests performed a mass in Latin while the nuns looked on like the rest of us. The strangeness of ritual performed in a dead tongue was beautiful in its way, but none of it so moving as the chant had been. Briefly, everything had become still; the voice in my head had quieted. If I were capable of faith, I thought, I would have felt it then. After that, I returned to observ-ing it all with respectful curiosity. When Communion was offered, I went up to take it. The last time I'd done so had been at my father's funeral, surrounded by family members unaware that I hadn't been raised in the Church. I knew as I walked to the altar that I wasn't properly qualified, but I went up anyway, hoping to recover the feeling I'd had when the chanting started. Nothing came of it. I received the little cardboard quarter in my hands, brought it to my mouth, and let it dissolve into mush on my tongue.

It was after 9:00 AM. when mass ended. Sophie would be awake, perhaps upset about my disappearance with her car, and my breakfast plan would be spoiled. Still, I wandered the grounds for a few minutes instead of going straight back to the parking lot. I was on the edge of some insight, and I couldn't take myself away. I pictured that beautiful young girl in her habit. If I could capture the sight of her, convey it to Sophie when I got home, she would understand. It would make a great story, she'd say.

So it would. As I wandered, I thought of writing something about that girl, about her motives for coming there. Certainly, it would be different from the empty scenes of literary parties and ironic conversation in my first book. I wanted to spend time in this place, to find out what life was like for her now, not just the small public portion at mass, but the private moments that together made her days.

Of course, I saw none of that. The women were cloistered away from eyes like mine. That was part of the point. What I saw instead was a kind of farm: two barns and beyond them the residential spaces. The women had filed out the back of the church after mass, and there was no sign of them now. One small building was open to the public, and I followed some of the other churchgoers into it.

It disappointed me to find a gift shop there, though I can't say why. Up front was a shelf of literature about the order, and I took a pamphlet to bring home with me. Beside the shelf sat a stack of mounted prints showing scenes from the abbey.

"Those are all painted by the sisters themselves," the woman behind the register said when she saw me looking through them.

I took a painting of the church from the pile and brought it to the register.

"Are you in the order?" I asked the woman.

"I just work for them."

"What is it like here? For them, I mean."

"The sisters are Benedictine," the woman said. "That means they follow the rule of Benedict: *ora et labora*. Prayer and work. The work depends on each woman's skills and her interests and her experience before coming here. It's mostly contemplative, you know. Lots of prayers and study. And they stay inside the enclosure."

"Do you think they're happy here?"

I don't know what made me ask her this, but she accepted the question as natural.

"Did you hear them this morning?" she asked.

"Yes, I did."

"Well, I imagine you'd have to be happy to make such joyful noise."

"I suppose you're right."

"Will that be all?" she asked.

"I think so."

"You don't want any cheese?"

She pointed to a dozen large wheels of cheese sitting behind the register.

"The sisters make them. They're sort of famous for it."

"Are they good?"

"Absolutely. And they make bread to go with it."

She handed me one of the wheels, letting me feel its

weight, its gratifying solidity. I liked the idea that these women, sequestered for ascetic contemplation, produced this round thing that found its purpose in the world they'd left behind. I remembered the meal I'd planned. I wouldn't be returning empty-handed. Perhaps the goal that had kept me at the abbey had been breakfast after all, not revelation.

Back in the car, I pulled out of the driveway and turned in the direction I'd been heading. I followed the curves up the hill. After another mile, the road swung around to intersect with the one I'd started on. I turned back toward the Manse, and in another ten minutes I was back. The dashboard clock read 9:40 AM when I turned off the car.

Everything was as I'd left it. I found a knife and a plate in the kitchen. The cheese let out a smell of satisfying pungency as I sliced through its rind. I brought two pieces of it upstairs with some bread. The door to Sophie's room was half open, and I called in to her, but no answer came. I gave a light knock before pressing into the room. The bed was empty, and I was about to leave and look for her somewhere else when I saw her on the floor. Right away I knew that something terrible had happened, but I was halfway across the room before I had any sense of how terrible. A halo of blood or bile surrounded her head on the floor, and her cheeks had gone a sickening gray. I dropped the plate and tried to shake her awake. When she didn't respond, I grabbed the phone from the bedside table and called for an ambulance. Then I sat down beside her and waited for help to come.

When I heard the sirens I went downstairs to direct the paramedics to her. There were three of them and they all rushed in, but their response when they got to her side told me everything. After that, things slowed down. I don't mean this metaphorically or impressionistically. I mean that the urgency was gone and the paramedics moved with tired deliberation. The time to hurry had passed. We were into the time that came next. Two of the men stood around, seeming embarrassed, while the third pressed his hands to various parts of Sophie's body. Then one of the onlookers came to me in the doorway.

"Your, ah, your." He spoke with a professional calm even as he struggled to find a name to put to her. "Your wife?" he hazarded.

"My friend."

"Your friend," he said, as though trying it out. Then he hit on something he preferred. "The young lady," he said with evident satisfaction. "The young lady. I'm afraid we're too late for her."

"She's dead?"

He turned his head, as though in disappointment at the poor taste I'd shown by putting the situation in such terms.

"Yes," he said.

"What happened?"

"I can't really say at this point. The police will be on their way to take a closer look at everything. In the meantime, we'd like you to wait downstairs."

Twenty minutes later two officers arrived in a single car with sirens off. They took dutiful notice of me where I sat on the porch with a cigarette, but they said nothing before meeting one of the paramedics in the doorway. The three conferred for a few minutes before one of the cops approached me.

"You're the one who called in the emergency?" he asked.

"Yes," I said. "My name is Charlie Blakeman."

"I'm Detective Sutton," he said. "Can I ask you for identification?"

I gave him my driver's license. The picture on it was almost fifteen years old, taken in high school, before I'd even met Sophie, but he hardly looked at it.

"What's your relationship with the victim?"

"I'm just an old friend from college. I came to visit for the weekend."

"All right," he said. "I'd like you to tell me about the two of you, about what happened."

How far back did he want me to go? How much would be necessary or even helpful? I said that we hadn't seen each other for years until she'd come to a party at my house in Manhattan a few weeks before, and that she'd invited me to visit for the weekend. He wrote in a continuous scribble, seeming to give equal weight to each word, not to value any one fact above another, making it impossible to know whether he found this history irrelevant or telling in some way. I told him that we'd both had quite a lot to drink the night before, that she'd left me to sleep in another room and gone off to bed. I didn't mention that we'd been together first. He kept writing, letting me go on with the story.

That morning, I said, I'd gone out for a drive, hoping to go into town to buy us breakfast, but I'd gotten lost and been gone from the house for a few hours. I knew this sounded improbable, but I didn't want to mention going to the abbey. I was saving that story for Sophie; it would spoil if I told it to anyone else first. I only repeated that I'd gotten lost and returned later than intended. Then I'd gone upstairs to look for her. When she wouldn't wake, I called 911.

He kept writing for a minute after I'd finished talking. I couldn't tell if he was still transcribing my words or adding

his own commentary about my demeanor or some incon-
sistency in what I'd said. Once he'd finished, he looked up
at me.

"Do you know who William Crane is?"

It was as though he'd only heard the things I hadn't
said.

"That's her father-in-law."

"She's married?"

'

He wrote all this down carefully.

"Was your friend suffering from any kind of emotional
difficulty?"

"She was pretty shaken up about Crane's death. Do
you mind if I ask where you got his name?"

He looked me over.

"It was on the bottle of pills she took."

"She took pills? What kind of pills?"

"We don't know that yet," he said. "So she was de-
pressed after her father-in-law died?"

"I don't know if I would call it depression. Like I told
you, she'd split up with her husband. She'd started drinking again, which she'd quit for years. But she didn't kill
herself, if that's what you mean. I'm sure of it."

He stopped taking notes and looked up. For the first
time since we'd started talking he seemed truly interested
in what I had to say.

"What makes you think that?"

"She's a Catholic," I said. "It's against her religion."

He seemed to think I was trying to make his job difficult with this remark, but he responded calmly.

"I'm Catholic myself. Suffice it to say she wouldn't be
the first of my coreligionists to contradict Church doc-
trine."

"My family is Catholic," I said, "and I wouldn't tell you this about any of them. But Sophie took it very seriously. She really believed. She would have been sending herself to hell."

"Okay," he said. He wrote a few more lines down. "Thanks for that. And do you know anything about these pills?"

"No."

"There were two empty bottles near the bed. It's possible that she'd been taking them to get to sleep, that there were just one or two left in each bottle, and she overestimated, things mixed with the alcohol, et cetera. Especially if she wasn't used to drinking."

He was saying all this for my sake. He'd already decided what had happened, though he hadn't even been inside.

"We'll figure this all out in the next few days. But I want to be honest with you. In my experience it's not easy to overdose accidentally on these kinds of prescriptions. I suspect she knew what she was doing."

He told me to wait a bit longer while he joined the others inside.

When they came out again, they brought Sophie with them, zipped up in a bag on the stretcher. I turned away as they loaded her into the ambulance. Officer Sutton stayed behind to talk with me. At the end of our conversation, he handed me his business card and took down my cell phone number.

"Thanks for your help," he said. "And I'm sorry for the loss. We're going to know a lot more within the next twenty-four hours. You should feel free to give us a call if anything occurs to you. We might have some more questions for you, so for the time being, you probably shouldn't go anywhere."

"I won't," I promised. He hardly needed to ask. There was nowhere left on earth for me to go.

5

THAT NIGHT SOPHIE slept uncomfortably but deeply. When the buzzer woke her in the morning, her neck was stiff where it had been pressed against the arm of the chair. She wondered how she'd look to whoever was on the other side of the door. Her clothes were wrinkled. Her hair, grown longer than she usually wore it, was pressed into an awkward part. Her watch said eight o'clock. She didn't expect hospice for hours.

Through the peephole she saw two men, one white and one black, both of them large. They didn't look unfriendly, but Sophie had no idea what kind of business they might have there. She put the chain lock on before opening the door wide enough to look out.

"Can I help you?" she asked.

"We're here to deliver the bed," one of the men answered.

"The bed?"

"Is there a patient here who needs a hospital bed?"

Sophie had imagined some kind of barrier or guardrail being installed for Crane. She hadn't thought they would bring an entirely new bed. She unlocked the chain and opened the door. Beside the men in the hall were several large boxes and a mattress. She stepped aside as they carried them into the apartment.

"Where do you want this set up?"

"In the bedroom, I suppose."

She led them there and turned on the lights. Crane didn't stir.

"Don't worry about him," Sophie said. "He's a heavy sleeper."

The men went about their work without another word, assembling a full hospital bed with a steel frame on wheels and a handheld electric adjuster like an old two-buttoned remote control. After they set it up, they showed her how to work the thing. Then one of the men looked over to Crane.

"We can move him if you want."

She considered this. He would feel helpless being handled by these men, but this wasn't her first concern. She hadn't bought diapers yet, and she wasn't sure if he'd made it cleanly through the night.

"Will you give me a moment to wake him?"

They retreated discreetly from the room. At the bedside Sophie met the mild stench of sweat and sleep, but nothing to indicate that he'd shit himself again. She shook him lightly until his eyes opened. He looked frightened and confused, as he had when she'd found him on the floor. In these moments it was impossible not to care for him, no matter how difficult he was when he was truly himself.

"Good morning," she said, trying to sound soothing.

"What is it?"

He might have been speaking about the world before his eyes.

"We're going to move you into another bed. It will only take a second. You'll be safer there, and more comfortable. You'll be able to sit up or put your legs up. And you won't fall out again."

She wasn't sure he still remembered his fall. She waited for him to respond, though she didn't need his consent for anything. He had no control over what happened to his body anymore. If she wanted him moved, he would be moved. He seemed to know as much, and he nodded feebly. She called the men back in, expecting them to help him up and walk him to the bed. Instead they put their hands beneath him and lifted, as though carrying another mattress. After setting him on the new bed, they pulled a sheet and blanket over him with an odd tenderness.

"You'll be very comfortable here," one of the men said.

When they'd left, Sophie stripped the now-empty bed and made it up with clean sheets from the closet. When she'd finished, she checked on Crane. He was awake but unresponsive, his face frozen in a look of defeat. He was in exactly the position he'd been fighting desperately all this time to escape: dying in a hospital bed. Now that he was settled in this new bed with its thick barriers, she could go about the day without worrying. But the point was precisely to worry over him, so she still spent the morning sitting in his room. Every few minutes she got up and stood at his side. She tried to make him take a drink, which he did only once.

While she watched him she thought about Tom and the fire like the memory of a bad dream. Perhaps she kept herself bound to Crane's side because she knew those folders were waiting in the other room, and she didn't want to hear the story they had to tell her.

When the woman from hospice came to relieve her, Sophie went to the pharmacy, where she bought a package of adult diapers and a large, soft sponge made for washing skin rather than dishes. She refilled the prescription for Crane's pills, though there were plenty left. She did it only for the convenience, she told herself, so that he wouldn't be left to suffer if they ran out at an awkward time.

Back in the apartment, she saw the woman out, gave Crane a pill, and sat in the living room. Having avoided them all day, she now went to the folders with urgency. She needed to prove what she already knew: that the police had made a mistake, that Crane was responsible. It was amazing how the stories proliferated, and how many of them he had saved. She was now on folder number three. Still she found only more references to "suspicion" falling on "the victim's son."

Before then, Tom had been treated as a victim himself, but now he was a relation at best. They never gave his name or provided a picture, but one article mentioned that he'd gone to live with an aunt out of state. These articles would sometimes mention, in a stray paragraph near the end, that Crane's condition was unchanged or that doctors were guarded but hopeful. Finally, near the end of the pile, came a piece that focused directly on Crane. "UM Professor Hurt in Fire Regains Consciousness." Below this headline it said that the police would interview Crane within the day. The next page in the folder was the first article that named Crane as a suspect. More precisely, it said that he had "claimed responsibility" for the fire.

Sophie moved quickly through the rest of the clips, which became shorter after that. They outlined the process of his confession, his plea deal with prosecutors, his release from the hospital into the custody of the police. The fourth folder ended with the start of his prison term. She felt no satisfaction from arriving at this inevitable end. The story still hung unresolved.

She went to the kitchen to eat and while she was there she poured a glass of scotch, which she took into the living room. Charlie's book sat on the coffee table. She picked it up and made a brief effort with it. But it seemed only slighter now. Her mind kept returning to the folders. She couldn't bear to go back through them, but she couldn't stop thinking of them, either. She decided to skip ahead, into the future, to see what Crane's life had been like since his release. Folder eight was filled with more recent newspaper clippings. She was relieved to see that they had nothing to do with the fire.

The first article was from the sports pages of a paper in New Jersey. This perplexed Sophie until she saw that it was about a local baseball game in which junior Thomas O'Brien had pitched a two-hit shutout. Beside the article ran a photo of Tom in his uniform, his bright face looking out from beneath the rounded bill of his baseball cap. Sophie had seen a photo much like this one on Beth's bureau. She lingered on her husband's face before moving through the rest of the pages. There were announcements of debate matches and school plays, human-interest pieces about community service done by the local church, all of them from two small papers covering a few towns in southern Jersey.

When she'd finished with the folder, Sophie checked on Crane and found him still asleep. She let herself out and walked downstairs. Lucia Ortiz answered after only one knock on her door.

"Sophie Crane," she said. "I thought I hear you in the halls."

"I came to take care of my father."

"How is he doing?"

"Not so well, I'm afraid."

"I pray for him every day," Lucia said. Seeing Sophie's worried expression, she added, "Is there something I can do to help you?"

"There might be," Sophie said. "It may sound like a strange request. But you mentioned that you and my father had both been living here for several years. Was he here when you moved to the building?"

"No," Lucia said. "He come a couple of years after I come."

"Do you remember when that was, exactly? I'm sorry to bother you with this, but it would be a real help to know. I'm trying to settle some of his business."

Lucia thought for a moment and then smiled.

"I know exactly, because my son graduated from high school that year. He helped Mr. Crane carry some things upstairs, and then later, in the fall, Mr. Crane helped us move his things out when he go to college." She counted to herself. "Almost twenty years. Time goes by. My son, he's a doctor now. Always talking of moving me out of here. Why do I want to move? I like it here."

"That's wonderful," said Sophie. "You must be very proud of him."

"You let me know if I can help more."

"Just keep praying for him. Keep praying for us all."

Back upstairs she refilled her glass and took it into the bedroom. Crane's eyes were closed, but his head shook back and forth as though in denial of something, and he let out a low list of moans. One hand was up near his face, clasping and unclasping but holding only air.

He might have been a beaten animal, knowing nothing of his suffering, only inhabiting it. And she was powerless to stop it. She could have shaken him from sleep, as though it were a bad dream he was suffering, but he would only wake into more pain. She wished to still him with a touch. Part of her wanted simply not to have to watch, not to know that what she saw was real. She knelt at his side, leaning against the bed frame as against a Communion rail, and she prayed for his ordeal to pass.

If Lucia's memory was correct, Crane had come to New York the year he got out of prison. It was as good a place as any to start a life over, but he would have known that Tom and Beth were just an hour away. She wasn't sure if the local Jersey papers had been delivered to Manhattan in those days. More likely he'd driven to get them. She imagined him even going to one of those baseball games, following Tom from a safe distance. What else had he done with his life? He would have had some job, of course, perhaps until he got sick, but it couldn't have been much of a career. All the evidence in the apartment suggested that he'd given the past twenty years to this story.

If he'd been following Tom, he'd been following her for as long as she'd shared her life with Tom. The things that he'd known on the first day they met, about her book and her conversion, were only the beginning. How many times had Crane seen her before the day she came to the hospital? Tom had thought he was gone, but he'd been there, almost close enough to touch, though still invisible.

"Get up, get up," she heard him say. She looked up, into his open eyes. He had not been so lucid in two days. "I know what you're doing," he said. "I didn't ask for it, and I don't want it. It's useless."

She stayed on her knees, looking at him.

"If it's useless, what difference does it make whether I do it or not?"

"Because I don't want to have to look at it," he said. "If you're going to pray, you can do it outside."

Still she didn't rise. Waiting for a store of generosity within her to meet his antagonism, she remembered those clippings and the shadow life he'd led.

"I'm sorry you're suffering."

"I'll be suffering either way. Your prayers don't do shit about it. They'll just make you feel better."

He closed his eyes and turned his head. His hand continued to reach out for nothing. He was well practiced, Sophie thought. He knew just how to use his pain as a weapon against her. But there was no mistaking that the pain was real, or that her prayers had no power over it.

She'd thought little over the years about the efficacy of prayer, though it was a fundamental matter of her faith. She prayed a great deal, but rarely *for* anything. She made prayers of thanksgiving and penitence and adoration, rather than prayers of petition or intercession. She sometimes prayed for the souls of her parents, but she didn't pray for God to intervene in the visible world.

No principle kept her from it. She wasn't among those who thought that God had better things to worry about than missing car keys or late trains. The moment that God stopped worrying about anything on earth, we stopped existing entirely. There was no stock of divine attention to be depleted. Guiding a vacant cab to a rich old woman in the rain on Park Avenue couldn't distract Him from starvation in some other corner of the world. Such intercessions just didn't occur to her in the moments when she knelt to speak with God.

But it was impossible to watch Crane struggle without praying for it to stop. So on this day she asked for something. Something not unreasonable, she thought. She might have asked, in that moment, for two decades to be erased, for that house in the woods to be restored and with it the family within. But she wasn't so ambitious. She prayed only that he not suffer through the days he had left. And then she knelt, watching the unmistakable proof that her prayer had not been answered.

He answers prayers in His own way, Sister Dymphna had told the initiates. The answers might be mysterious to us. You couldn't ask God to help you make your appointment and expect Him to reconfigure time and space to meet this preference. It would be childish to think that God must not exist, or must not be good, merely because He refused to conform the world to your own will. This had satisfied her at the time, but now it seemed inadequate. What did it mean to say that God answered prayers, if He chose which ones were worth answering? Or if His answer was so oblique that it was no answer at all? Simpler to say that God answered every prayer, but that sometimes the answer was no. That He made the world do as He wished, that if your wishes met His, your prayers were answered.

Why should Bill Crane be the one who put these matters into question for her? What was it about his suffering, above all the suffering the world held, that made it unconscionable to her? Was she objecting, at heart, to bearing witness to it? She had chosen to come to this place. He hadn't asked her there, and he didn't want forgiveness. He didn't even want her to stay. She had chosen to go through his files, to learn things that Tom had kept from her for years. She had chosen to knock on Lucia Ortiz's door, to confirm a suspicion that might as easily have been left unconfirmed. Not to help anyone, but because she'd wanted to make sense of the story.

She decided to find a church in the area that held mass during the hour after Sarah arrived.

Now she stood, placing a hand awkwardly against the hot, wet skin of his face. He turned back to her and opened his eyes but said nothing. He seemed already to have forgotten their earlier exchange.

"I'll get you some pills," she said.

Sophie filled a glass of water in the bathroom and brought it along with the painkillers back to his bed. Using the handheld control, she sat him up. He tried to reach for the pills, but his hands were shaking and wouldn't obey, so he leaned his head forward and opened his mouth. She placed two of the oblong white pills on his tongue. If they could keep his pain at bay, perhaps those pills were her answered prayer. She lifted the glass to his lips and poured the water down his throat.

Before he'd finished swallowing, Crane set his head back and closed his eyes. Relief couldn't possibly have come that soon, but the mere anticipation had given him some peace. She pulled the chair to the side of the bed and sat watching him. She didn't need to kneel. He couldn't know what was passing through her heart, and he couldn't change it if he did. She watched his body settle, his breathing become less labored. His hands fell back to his side. Without thinking, Sophie reached out for one and held it in her own. If he was conscious of her touch, he made no sign of it.

Did she make any difference at all to him? She suspected not. But she wasn't sure she needed him to need her there. That might not be the meaning of her work. Was it selfish then, this reaching for his hand, this desire that life be met by life? Was it for his sake or her own that she wanted to save his soul?

His soul. Had she said it out loud, he would have laughed at the word. Or spat on it. What would she tell him, if asked to explain the notion? If one thought of the soul as something that lived in the body like a kind of prisoner, but that wasn't finally dependent upon it, where was his soul while his body suffered in front of her? Did it suffer also? Or was his body losing its grip on it? Had it escaped? But then, what *was* in his still-living body, what animated it, such as it was, if not his soul? And where could his soul be found, if not in his body, while his body still lived?

She was interrupted in these thoughts when Crane called out. The sound seemed at first an odd corruption of his own name, as if the word had been caught in his throat and deformed on the way up, or spoken in a foreign tongue. He seemed to be asserting his continued presence in the world. She looked up, still holding his hand in hers, and waited for him to speak again.

Pills, it might have been. Not Bill. Though even this wasn't quite it.

"I can give you more in another two hours."

He shook his head from side to side, slowly but still forcefully. The pained look on his face might have been merely the effect of movement, or it might have been his disgust at her refusal. He spoke the awkward imperative again, and it came to her, in the instant before he repeated himself, what he had actually said, so that the words when they returned emerged not from him but from some place within her.

"Kill me."

She looked into his face, which had now gone blank, and she thought that he was slipping away again. She hoped so. Then she might pretend she hadn't heard. The burden might be passed. But there was life in his eyes, which darted from her face to the bottle of painkillers still in her other hand, trying to direct her.

"I won't," she told him, trying to sound certain. "Put it out of your head."

He seemed to do just that. He seemed in fact to absent himself entirely, leaving her alone in the room. He didn't know what he was saying, she thought. He wasn't capable of making such a request in this state. But death was what he'd wanted all along. Dying had been the plan that she'd spoiled the first time she entered his life. He'd needed someone to sign a form at the hospital and set him free. He didn't want to be saved. He wanted to be left to die.

Now he slept, and she stood up. As she pulled her sweating hand free from his, her fingers tingled sharply with a kind of mock pain, as if to remind her what suffering really was. She went into the kitchen with no real purpose except to escape from him. She fixed herself a scotch with two cubes of ice and drank it slowly while she wept over the sink.

What had she meant when she prayed for his ordeal to be over? What could she possibly have been asking for, except that he be taken from the world? And if she could ask for such a thing for him, why could he not ask for it himself? He was asking her to answer her own prayer.

When the drink was done, Sophie stood dazed with the empty glass in her hand, feeling herself empty beside it. She made another, adding water to it out of an inexplicable sense of propriety. She brought it out to the living room, where she sat on the couch.

There was a world inside the world, like the secret station beneath City Hall. Behind the visible lay the true nature of things. In that secret world, things were free. Perhaps the body was not a cage that held the soul, but a hand that gripped it like a cane, appearing to guide it, to command it, but all the while dependent upon it, gripping it all the tighter the more that it needed it, finally letting it go.

But Crane wasn't asking for his soul to be released. He wasn't asking her to usher him from one nature into another, from this world to the other. He wanted an end. He wanted no longer to exist. Sophie couldn't blame him. If she thought such a thing were possible, she might want it, too. But it wasn't so. Once you had been made to exist, you had no choice but to do so forever. There was no escape for anyone.

The torment he felt now would be followed only by greater torment. But this would be so either way. She'd given up the thought that he might repent and confess. If he was damned, what difference would it make to him whether his damnation commenced now, or in a week, or in a month? Soon enough he would be outside of time.

She wasn't sure how much she'd had to drink, and so she wasn't sure if she should be taking the pill, but she couldn't have peace without it. She needed a long, dreamless sleep. She climbed into Crane's empty bed, the fourth place she'd slept in four nights, feeling she would never find a resting place all her own.

"How is your father today?" Sarah asked in the morning.

Sophie couldn't say, exactly, since she'd only just woken up at the sound of the buzzer. It seemed to her that they ought to establish some intimacy, given the circumstances, given what they shared between them, but she was unable even to begin a conversation with the woman.

"He's been struggling," she answered.

Entering the apartment, Sarah noticed immediately the glass of scotch sitting on the table, as if such noticing were part of her job. She made no mention of it, only letting her eyes rest long enough that there be no mistake. Sophie wanted to explain that it was there from the night before, but that would mean admitting that she had spent the whole morning asleep, and the judgment would remain unchanged.

"I'll go check on him now," Sarah said. "You must be ready for a break."

"Yes," Sophie said. "It's been difficult."

A day before she would not have admitted such a thing.

Back at home—for the first time since leaving, she thought of her apartment as home—she could have gone online to find the schedule of a neighborhood church, but Crane had no computer. Just by wandering, she might have found a church with a mass at 11:15 or 11:30. But she'd be left to scramble back before Sarah's time was over, confirming that she wasn't a responsible caretaker. In the end, she returned to the Spanish church, although it was empty at that hour.

She headed straight for the pew in the front where the women had been two mornings earlier. She knelt and crossed herself, letting the silence echo through her for a moment. Then she tried to begin. Never since prayer had come into her life had she felt at such a loss when trying to pray. She didn't know what to do with the image she now had of this man, following his son through life. Even when she banished this thought, a picture of an old man, shaking in the hospital bed that he'd wanted so badly to avoid, replaced it. The pills would have worn off during the night. She hoped that Sarah had given him more, until she remembered that she still had the painkillers.

In her pocket, Sophie's fingers worried over the pills. As long as he was suffering without them, it was impossible to think of anything else. And it was impossible, as long as she was thinking of it, not to want his suffering to end. She prayed for it, though she knew what it meant to pray for such a thing.

Stepping back out into the light, her eyes balking at the sight of the noon sun, she couldn't place the source of her tears. They felt like tears of rage, even of defiance. But rage against whom? Defiance of what? She had been defeated, but she couldn't name the adversary that had won.

Sarah stood over Crane in the bedroom, wiping his face with a towel, her hand describing a figure eight, down from his forehead to his cheek, across the upper lip to the chin and back around. She continued the motion even as she looked up at Sophie. They stood in silent opposition. Then Sarah looked at her watch.

"You still have another fifteen minutes," she said. "I'm sure you'll want some rest."

"That's all right," Sophie answered. "You can go."

Sarah hesitated before setting the sponge down. She looked at Bill, who gave no notice to either of them.

"I'll wait in the other room. In case you need anything."

Sophie took her place at Bill's bedside and found him unmoving but awake, his eyes open and darting about in frightening contrast to the stillness of his body.

"How are you feeling?" she asked.

She couldn't tell if he intended the sounds that he made to cohere into words, or to be expressive in some more direct and urgent way. He seemed to be returning to infancy, in the etymological sense: he had exited the stream of language. They continued the exchange they'd started that morning, but he was so much more persuasive now that he'd given up words.

He was there, above all, to challenge her; he existed as a challenge. It was terrible to think about him as he lay suffering, as though his pain were more real for her than it was for him. For there was nothing of him held apart from the suffering to honor it; he could only live within it. Her purpose was to witness it.

Sophie walked back outside, where Sarah sat on the couch.

"I appreciate your dedication," she said. "But really, you can go now."

"All right," Sarah answered after a moment. "I'll be back tomorrow."

"Actually, we won't need you anymore." Sophie had not come into the room expecting to tell her this. "I'm going to take care of things from here."

"You're sure? You'll need a bit of help, at least."

It occurred to Sophie for the first time that this woman's livelihood was at stake. Her interest in his care had a simple purpose: she wanted to keep her job.

"Quite sure."

"I'm not authorized to cancel the arrangement," Sarah said. "You're going to have to call the service."

"That's fine."

As Sarah gave her a card with the number to call, Sophie felt relieved that she'd been unable to establish any connection with the woman.

"Thank you," she said finally. "I do appreciate your help."

"Good luck," Sarah said, making no effort to hide her disapproval.

Turning from the door, Sophie saw the living room as Sarah must have seen it, the papers on the floor, the half-finished scotch still sitting on the table near the couch. She picked up the glass and took a slow sip. The ice cubes had long ago melted, and the drink wasn't as strong as it had been the night before. Sophie finished it quickly. She took out her cell phone and made the cancellation call. Having made the decision, she wanted to act on it before she changed her mind.

"Were you unhappy with our service?" the man on the phone asked her.

"No, nothing like that," Sophie said. "In fact, I want to make sure you know how happy we were with Sarah's work. I just want to take care of things myself."

It made no difference to him. He asked because he was compelled to ask. Then he went about the rest of the steps. It was all over very quickly. Whatever was to happen next would happen only between Sophie and Crane. She had sent away the rest of the world.

She returned to Bill's bedside, placed two pills on his tongue, and lifted the water to his lips. They were alone now. No one would be coming for them.

So began the last days.

Sometimes it seemed that he wasn't there inside, that she was watching a husk from which he had already escaped. But he had moments, sudden bursts of startling lucidity, when he came back fully into himself. She wondered if these times felt to him like small islands of consciousness surrounded by hours of floating, if he had the sensation of coming up for air, or if those brief moments were all that existed for him, the stretches between them striking him as dreams or not at all.

He would say something that seemed another piece of nonsense, but which after a moment Sophie realized referred to a conversation they'd had during his last bout of intelligibility. Or else he just named something in front of him, a color or an object, as if remembering that such things had names and greedy to participate in naming. Or as if a word could be a bridge between the speaker and the thing it named, and this was his way of pulling himself across that bridge, back into the world.

Each time he spoke he let her know that he still wanted it to end, that she had the power to make it so and refused. One of these periods lasted far longer than the others, so that for a time she was given to believe that the decline might have stopped. For the better part of three days, he spent every waking moment calling out for his own death. On the last day she had to go into the other room; she couldn't listen anymore. That night she slept on the couch, checking him at points but retreating in fear even when she found him quietly asleep.

He was suffering to save her soul. It was for her own sake, not for his, that she refused to intervene, when she might end his ordeal at any moment. How did it serve him, to make him live? What did his suffering win him? Where was the nobility in prizing her soul at the cost of his suffering?

She had for a time been much taken with the contrarian argument about Judas Iscariot. Briefly, it went: Jesus needed Judas to betray him in order to save us all. This made him the most selfless, perhaps the greatest, of all the apostles, because he was the one who could never be saved, and still he played the role it was given him to play.

Sophie did the opposite. When Bill fell back into confusion, she gave him protein drinks, which she knew he would accept in that state. She didn't want him starving to death. It would be too painful. This was absurd given the circumstances, but every instinct in her pushed toward the preservation of life. Why was this? Shouldn't he, who thought there was nothing outside this life, prize what was here above everything? Shouldn't she have been the one eager to shepherd him out of the visible world?

While he slept, she entered these thoughts into her note-book. She wasn't trying to tell a story. What mysteries remained about Bill Crane she didn't want to solve. She wrote now to save herself. She needed these thoughts to leave her head, and putting them on the page was the sim-plest way of being rid of them. She needed to pass them on, to put the burden on another. She was no longer thinking quite straight. She took two sleeping pills each night, since she woke in a terrible sweat when she took only one, her heart pounding from dreams she couldn't remember. Even when she took two she woke eventually with the feeling of having had an unsettled sleep.

One day she realized that a week had passed since she'd last left the apartment. Abstractly considered, she would have liked to leave. But there was no one else to sit vigil over him. She hadn't imagined he would last so long. After emptying the scotch she found another bottle beneath the sink, hidden among the cleaning supplies like contraband. She was careful not to mix it with the sleeping pills, so she drank only during the day and took the pills at night.

The day she discovered the second bottle was the day she gave up on prayer. Not for his sake. She would have happily prayed forever against his will, just as she fed him and changed him against his will, kept him alive against his will. But she was no longer capable of it. She would remain incapable for as long as he lived. The best she could hope was that the capability would return upon his passing.

She held out for two days after that. Then she set him free.

6

AFTER THE POLICE and the ambulance had left, I stood in the driveway looking at Sophie's car, which had survived another generation of Wilders. I guessed it belonged to Tom now, like the Manse itself. He'd probably sell them both, since it was hard to imagine him making use of either. For now, they were still mine to use, and I decided to go for another drive.

The road into town was so clearly marked that I couldn't believe I'd missed it a few hours before. I wondered what would have been different if I'd made that turn the first time. I didn't know when Sophie had taken the pills, when she'd fallen out of bed. It had probably all been decided before I left the house that morning. But perhaps I could have saved her if I had made the trip I'd set out to make and returned an hour earlier.

In town I bought cleaning supplies and enough food to last another week. I wasn't sure how long the police expected me to stay, but it would be at least another few days before anyone in New York wondered where I was. Max and I kept different hours, slipping away from time to time without explanation. At one of his parties, someone might ask why I wasn't around, and Max would shrug. "Am I my cousin's keeper?" he would say. I spoke with my mother no more than once a week, so a few days without word wasn't remarkable. I could disappear from my life; no one would really notice I was gone.

Who would notice Sophie's disappearance? Our meeting on the sidewalk suggested she hadn't been speaking much with Tom. The police would call him soon, if they hadn't already. He would then tell his aunt and others, and they would begin making arrangements. But for now it was possible that I was the only one who knew. If it had happened before she'd appeared on Gerhard's couch, I don't know who would have thought to tell me. At best, I might have been included on an e-mail list that received a message from Tom announcing the time of the funeral. Or I'd run into an old classmate on the street who would ask, "Did you hear about Sophie Wilder? Weren't you two close?"

But it hadn't happened that way, because she had come looking for me to say good-bye. All the time I'd spent thinking of her, she'd been thinking of me, too. She'd wanted for us the same life that I wanted, even if she didn't think it was possible. As I put the food away in the kitchen cupboard, I imagined this life, and somehow I believed it wasn't too late for us to save each other. I brought a bucket, a mop, and a bottle of soap up into Sophie's room. I felt oddly unmoved by the sight of the red-brown crescent on the floor, until I started going over it with the mop. I cried as the color faded, but I kept working at it until the stain was gone.

I changed the sheets on Sophie's bed, where I spent the rest of the day.

In the morning, Detective Sutton called my cell phone.

"Is there any news?" I asked.

"Not much," he said. "But we'd like to follow up with you. Just run through a few more questions."

"That's fine."

"Where are you now?"

"I'm at the house."

"Ms. O'Brien's house?"

"Yes."

"You just moved right in?"

"I thought you wanted me to stay."

"Stay in the area," he said. "In the country. Stay available. I didn't mean in the house."

"I'm sorry, I misunderstood. I hope it doesn't cause any problems."

"No, no," he said. "I suppose you're entitled."

"Well, I'm here now."

"All right. That's fine. I'll be over in about an hour."

We sat on the porch, going through things. He asked me how long it had been since I'd seen Sophie before that week. I couldn't say for sure.

I told him about the wedding we'd both gone to about a year before. I'd danced drunkenly with Sophie, holding her close. "Are you happy?" I whispered to her. She didn't answer but stiffened in my arms. We danced until the end of the song. It was followed by something faster, and everyone stormed the dance floor to jump around in amorphous groups. The crowd absorbed and separated us, and we didn't speak again for the rest of the night. I kept drinking. Eventually I convinced one of the bridesmaids—a high school friend of the bride's whom I'd never met before and never did again—to come up to my hotel room for some mild messing around before we both passed out. By the time I woke up, I hardly remembered the incident with Sophie. I hadn't thought about it since.

"So you'd say it was about a year?" Sutton asked, smiling slightly.

"I'm sorry," I said. "I'm a bit out of sorts, and I'm not really sure what's relevant and what isn't."

"Might as well err on the side of inclusion."

After that, he asked me all the same questions he'd asked before. He didn't seem to have any new angle of approach; he just wanted me to repeat everything.

"Has something happened?" I asked. "Is there something in particular that you're trying to find out?"

"Not really," he said. "Cause of death was definitely an overdose. I know you don't want to hear this, but I'm afraid it's unlikely to be ruled accidental. There were just too many pills in her system. We wanted to do some follow-up, since the timing lends itself to some suspicion."

"The timing?"

"About a month ago Mrs. O'Brien made some substantial changes to her will."

I didn't think people our age even had wills, perhaps because I didn't have anything to leave behind.

"Well," I said, "her husband left her. Maybe it made her rethink certain things."

"So she didn't tell you anything about this?" he asked. He gave a clipped wave at the front door, as though welcoming me.

I leave it to you.

"The house?"

"The house," he said. "And a small trust to pay for its upkeep. And the car. Everything else—there's a fair amount still left from her parents' estate and royalties from a book she wrote—was divided between her husband, a few churches, something called the Manhattan Speech Pathology Center, and a woman named Elizabeth O'Brien. The husband's mother, I guess?"

"His aunt."

"And you didn't know about this?"

"She didn't tell me. I mean, not really. She told me I could stay for a while, that she wasn't going to be using the house. But there was never any talk about wills or anything like that."

This seemed to satisfy him.

"Of course, on a certain level it makes plenty of sense," Sutton said. "If she knew she was going to do this and didn't want these old family assets to go to her estranged husband. But it's a bit odd that it would be just these two items. There's an investment portfolio, which the lawyers tell us is worth more than the house and the car combined, and a lot of that goes to him. So it's not just about wanting to keep things from the guy."

"Her parents are here," I said.

"They're here?"

"Their ghosts." I knew this wasn't the time for such propositions, so I tried to explain what I meant in rational terms. "The house and the car were the last things she shared with her parents. She would want them to go to someone who would hold on to them, make use of them."

"All right. Do you have anything else to add?"

"I still don't think she did it on purpose."

"Because of her religion?"

"She wouldn't send herself to hell."

He seemed to consider this now not as an officer of the law, but as a man speaking with a confused boy.

"Unless she was going there either way."

He'd made himself uncomfortable with this speculation, and he stood up from the chair. He paced the length of the porch before returning to me.

"Did the two of you have a fight or anything? Is there something that might have happened between you the other night to precipitate something like this?"

It would have been easy enough for them to tell that we'd slept together just a few hours before she died.

"No," I said. "Whatever happened had nothing to do with me."

This was true. It had never had anything to do with me.

"Well, I think that's it for now. We're probably going to close everything up on this pretty soon, but we may want to speak with you again. You don't have to stay, just answer your phone."

"All right," I said. "And what about the house?"

"That's not really my area. The lawyer executing the will should be in touch with you soon. These things take some time to sort out, but assuming the husband doesn't plan to contest it, you'll be able to start making arrangements before too long. Beyond that, I can't really say."

I walked him to his car and watched him leave. Once he was gone, I stood in the driveway, wondering what to do now. The wind had picked up, and it rattled the screen door before passing into the house, over the floorboards, the stairs.

It was a short way from town to the main southern route. Within a few minutes I was on the road to New York. I hadn't done much highway driving before, and I would have been terrified if I'd cared enough to be. Instead, I felt the same anger toward the car that Sophie had described to me. It wasn't a gift she had left me, but a burden. What was

I expected to do with it? It would have been very easy to give up control of the car, to take my hands from the wheel, freeing it to drift toward the median, destroying itself and me with it—destroying the whole story, really, since I alone remained to tell it. What kept me from it was not any great desire to persist, but the feeling that Sophie had a plan.

I parked a few blocks from Washington Square and walked to Gerhard's house. It felt as though I'd been gone for a very long time. I imagined a scene out of a dream or fable: the house occupied by strangers who would treat me as an interloper and tell me that they'd been living there for years, since those two strange cousins disappeared all that time ago. Instead, I saw Max coming down the stairs with his suitcase in his hand.

"Groucho Marx–grade timing," he said when he saw me standing near the door. "Where the fuck have you been?"

So then he had noticed that I was gone.

"Something terrible has happened," I told him.

"No shit," he said. "Daddy's home."

Max pointed to the couch, where Gerhard sat slumped over, his head in his hands. It had been months since I'd seen him.

"Welcome back," I called to him.

He didn't respond.

"Spoiled children," he said, to no one in particular. "A bunch of spoiled children."

Then he walked out of the room, into the kitchen, and in his absence I saw the aquarium. One of the glass panels was shattered, and the water and the fish were gone. A piece of the wrought-iron frame that should have been holding the missing panel was bent back into the tank. The damage was not the result of casual work; someone had committed real violence against the thing.

Max had set his suitcase down and was heading back up the stairs.

"Come on, Charlie," he said. "I need you to give me a hand."

"What the fuck happened?" I asked him on the second floor.

"Tough to say for sure," Max answered. "I had a few chums over last night. Nothing too involved. But there was an altercation. Funny thing for this crowd, as I don't need to tell you. Not really men of action. The best lack all conviction, and so on. But Rick Tanner threw Jeff into the fish tank."

"Jesus."

"It didn't seem that bad at the time."

"They fucking totaled it."

"I'm not going to argue that the optics are good, hindsight-wise. I'm saying how it seemed to us at the time. You're going to have to trust me on that, since you weren't here. Which, we could have used you around. Anyway, I had every intention of cleaning things up in the morning. But it seems that the water leaked out of the tank overnight."

"Leaked? They smashed the thing open."

"Which certainly explains the leak. The problem is that the fish don't do well without water. Not an insurmountable problem. That is, the water problem certainly proved insurmountable for the fish. I mean more that the fish problem need not have been insurmountable for us. Except that Gerhard arrived this morning from some gutturally-articulated metropolis in the Benelux."

He was enjoying it all, in his way. Not that he would have wished it to happen, but he was glad he could at least get a good performance out of it.

"Max," I said.

"I know, I know." He waved me back to silence. "A little improbable in its timing, the return of Gottlieb. All I can say is that's how it happened. When you write it into the follow-up, you'll be free to make adjustments for the sake of plausibility."

"Max," I said again, and this time he fell quiet. "I can't have this conversation right now."

"That's for sure," Max answered. "He wants us out effective immediately. He said those fish were the most important thing in his life. I told him that if this was true, he ought to have visited them more often. Which went about how you'd expect. So: the world is all before us. Hand in hand, with wandering steps and slow. I'm headed up to the *pater familias* tonight. There's room for you, of course, though I guess you'll want to see your mom."

As he said that, I very much did.

"Sophie's dead," I told him.

A strange thing happened, then. Max's mask collapsed, and the hidden thing that lay beneath it was laid bare. The last time I'd seen this had been when my father died, and it was awful to watch. So much of Max's act depended on his commitment to it, on the understanding that nothing would ever truly penetrate. However much this exasperated, it also comforted. Once Max broke down, there could be no question that the loss was real.

"What happened?"

"They're not really sure," I said. "She died in her sleep."

"I'm sorry," said Max. "I know how important she was to you."

"We hadn't been close in years."

"So much the worse."

Nearly everything in the house belonged to Gerhard. I had only clothes and books to pack. I took as many as one bag would fit and left the rest behind. I said I'd come back once Gerhard had calmed down, but I suspected already that I would never return. I might have explained that I hadn't been there when the accident happened, that I would have saved the fish somehow if I could have. But who can really say what I would have done differently if I'd been there?

Downstairs, Gerhard stood crying in front of the aquarium. The sight of him, this man who had been so generous to us in his absence, set free all the despair I'd been feeling. We had been given something beautiful, asked only to watch over it. We'd been careless, and now it was all in ruin.

"Tomorrow, I'll start looking for a place," Max said as we walked out. "I'm sure we could find something nearly as big if we looked in Brooklyn."

"I'm leaving town for a while," I answered.

"Right on," he answered after a moment. "Morgan might be moving out of the loft on West Broadway, so the guys will be looking for someone to take his room. That should work out pretty well."

"Sounds good."

We were walking along the south end of the park.

"Do you want a ride uptown?" I asked.

"You going to treat me to a cab?"

"I've got Sophie's Jaguar."

"Jesus, Charlie. You stole her car?"

"She left it to me."

We drove in silence to my uncle's building on the Upper West Side. I double-parked and got out to help unload Max's bags.

"I might not see you for a while," I said.

"Getting away will be good for you," he said. "You can get back to work."

"I think I might."

"Do you know where you're headed?"

"I have some ideas."

"Charlie," he told me. "I'm sorry I ruined things between the two of you."

"It was all a long time ago."

"I know. And I've been sorry about it for a long time." He surprised me then by pulling me into a hug. "I love you, Charlie."

"I love you, too," I said. We stood in each other's arms while the doorman brought Max's bags into the lobby.

Driving through Central Park to my mother's apartment, I remembered weekends growing up, when Max and I and our fathers would play two-on-two basketball. Max was always a little bit bigger, a little stronger, and since our dads were both indifferent players, he and my uncle would win game after game. I would start to get frustrated, then, and Max would ease off defending me in the post, or take a quick, lazy shot that he knew was out of his range. This would only infuriate me more, because I wanted to beat him at his best. At some point, as we grew up, Max came to suppress this natural protectiveness toward me, knowing how I hated it.

It had been a long time since I'd come uptown to see my mother. I tried to do it once a month, but it didn't work out that way. I had plenty of time in those days, so there was really no excuse. I took for granted that she would be home, though I didn't know much about how she spent her days. I let myself into the apartment and heard the television in her room. She was lying in bed with a glass of wine, watching one of those forensic police procedurals in which some washed-up movie star spends an hour looking at semen under a microscope.

"Hey, Chazzie," she said when she saw me in the doorway. "What a nice surprise."

She didn't seem especially pleased.

"Hi, Mom. Sorry to sneak up on you."

I tried to say more as she got up from bed and came over to me, but the words wouldn't come.

"What's the matter?" she asked.

"Sophie's gone," I said.

"She's gone? I didn't know she was back."

"I mean she's dead."

My mother reached out to run her hands through my hair, a familiar gesture from my childhood. She'd done this often in the days when my father was dying, and I remembered how inadequate it had seemed to me then, as if anything in her power would have been sufficient to the time. She withdrew her hands and looked at me, wobbly and damp-eyed.

"When did it happen?"

"A couple of days ago."

"I'm so sorry."

She seemed to want me to release her from feeling too much about this girl she half remembered, who'd come to stay with us a few times years ago.

"It happened in her sleep."

"Why don't I make us a pot of coffee?"

We walked together into the hallway, and she saw the bag I'd brought uptown.

"Have you come to stay for a while?"

"No," I said. "I'm leaving town, and I wanted to say good-bye."

Once we were settled around the kitchen table, coffee mugs in hand, she asked, "How are you doing with this?"

"I'm lonely," I said.

"Me, too," my mother said.

I don't know why this struck me as it did. It was natural that a widow whose only child never visited should feel that way. I should have known all along that there had been someone whose suffering I could have done something about.

"I should come by more often."

"It's hard for you up here," she said. "And you have your life to live."

"I could stay for a little while. I don't really have to leave town right away."

"It wouldn't make much difference."

She was right. I was too late. We sat there together in the sad recognition that the time when we might have been a comfort to each other had passed, that we had both failed a long time ago.

"I never understood why things didn't work out between the two of you," she said. "I always liked Sophie."

"So did I."

We stayed up talking through most of the night, not about Sophie but about my dad. We told stories from my childhood, stories we'd both carried with us without ever thinking to express them to one another. My mother told me stories from before then, ones I'd never heard, that perhaps only she had known.

"He had an old cardigan," she said. "And he used to tuck you into it and sit for hours, reading while you slept."

The understanding that we couldn't fix each other's problems, that we were no longer expected to try, brought us closer than we'd been in years. At the end of the night,

I walked her back to her room. I left her there and spent a last night in my childhood bed.

Traffic kept me in the city longer than I wanted the next morning. Still uncertain behind the wheel, I watched all the signs carefully and drove with the perpetual sense that I'd missed a turn somewhere. I couldn't escape the feeling that I'd been on the road too long. But the exit came eventually, and I drove through town to the house. It didn't belong to me yet, I knew. Perhaps it never would, if Tom chose to create difficulties. But in the meantime, I knew that no one would keep me from staying there.

I stood in the driveway with my hand on the car's hood, feeling the living warmth beneath it. In front of me, the house sat waiting. Instead of going inside, I walked around back, beyond the pool to the work shed. The padlock on the door was open. It might have been that way for years, or Sophie might have left it unlocked in one of her last acts. There was a small wooden desk inside, and on it sat two marble notebooks, the kind we'd both used at school. There was also a lamp on the desk, and a chair beside it. Beneath the chair sat a pile of the same notebooks and a second pile of perhaps a half dozen manila folders, each with a number on it. There were also a few books, none of them familiar to me. Otherwise, the room was bare. The morning sun floated through the small oval window, illuminating the dust I'd unsettled with my arrival. I took a seat in the little room that Sophie and her father had built with their four hands.

Once it was too late to save anyone, even myself, I started to write.

7

CRANE ACCEPTED THE pills two at a time. His face showed no recognition that Sophie was granting his wish. If he felt anything, it may have been resentment that his wish remained hers to grant or not. He let out a string of short burps as he swallowed the pills but gave no other sign of their effect. She wasn't sure how many it would take, so she fed them to him until he stopped opening his mouth for more. Then she set the bottle down and waited.

His breathing gave way to short, desperate pleas for air. Between each one he remained completely still. Each breath seemed, in the moment that followed, to have been his last. The time separating his gasps grew longer. Every time she felt that the spirit had left, it fought to announce itself again. She already knew that she'd made a terrible mistake—had known it even as she'd done the thing—but there was no way now of undoing it.

Then it was over.

Sophie saw no difference between this new stillness and the stillnesses that had preceded it, so she waited a long time before she was certain that another breath wouldn't come. She had never watched a person die before. There had been two of them in the room, and now she was alone. Strange how it had come to pass: not a violent rending of life from the body, but a slow unbinding of spirit and matter.

For years after her parents' deaths, Sophie had dreamed of violent ends. She saw the accident as it happened. She was inside the car with them. She didn't think of it as imagining but as watching; she saw it, she thought, just as it had been. Her father had had a drink or two, no more, and the warmth of those drinks had put him in mind to take a hand from the wheel and place it on his wife's knee. He wasn't speeding, or not irresponsibly so. Then something happened to make him lose grip of the car, to make the car lose grip of the road, and they were spinning wildly toward two thick elms.

In some dreams it was her very presence in the car that did it. Her father caught sight of her watching, and he turned his attention from the road to question her. She came to him as an angel of death. She was in the car because of what had to happen next. He took his other hand from the wheel to fulfill what her presence made necessary. She stayed with them as the car skidded off the road, as it flipped over, even to the moment when it struck the first tree. But then she was expelled. There was a line she couldn't will herself across. She'd never seen their death.

Bill's hands were clasped and settled on his chest as though they had been placed in a model of repose. If someone had wanted to assure her that she'd given him peace, they would have made her picture his body just as it was then. But it meant nothing. What was this body now, that it could be said to have peace? Whose were those restful hands? What remained of him had passed to the invisible world. Crane would find no rest.

Sophie kneeled alone beside the pile of flesh that Bill Crane had left behind and tried again to pray, as though the end of his suffering presence in the world had lifted whatever barrier had kept her from prayer. But even now she was unable to speak. Something more than his suffering had kept her silent in those days. Her belief had not been shaken, but she felt herself outside of God's attention. She had trespassed in His domain—the place where life was extended or withheld. She could have prayed for Crane's soul, but it was too late for that. He had died unrepentant, and there was no interceding for him now. She could have prayed to be forgiven, but the time for this too seemed past. She had known what she was doing as she did it. If he should surprise her now with another breath, if this mute stillness before her was to reawaken into life and go on, she would continue feeding him the pills. *Why died I not from the womb? why did I not give up the ghost when I came out of the belly?*

Anyone coming upon them would have understood the picture: a man just gone from the world and his child beside him in tears. She had told enough people in the past weeks that she was his daughter to start believing it to be in some way true. But she didn't mistake the meaning of her tears. She wasn't crying over him. The loss she felt was of something else entirely.

Once she had given up on prayer, she went into the other room to call hospice, as though Bill might overhear her announcing his death.

"This is Sophie Crane," she said. "My father just died."

The man who answered put her on hold to look up the name.

"You cancelled your service," he said when he came back on the line.

"Yes," Sophie said.

"I'm afraid we can't do anything for you. I can give you the name and number of a funeral director in the neighborhood."

"That would be great."

"It's nonsectarian," he added, "so it doesn't matter what religion your family practices."

Once the men from the funeral home were on their way, it occurred to Sophie for the first time that she could be in trouble. An autopsy or some kind of investigation might reveal what she'd done. She went back to the bedroom and took all the pill bottles from the floor. She put them into her bag, which sat near the bed.

But the men asked no questions at all, not even about the cause of death. He had not been so old, but he had been very sick, and there was nothing remarkable about his passing. Now that he was gone, it was their job to handle what remained. There were four of them, all wearing dark colors and the placidly sympathetic faces of professional mourners. She imagined them on call somewhere an hour earlier, playing cards or restlessly smoking cigarettes while they waited to be summoned to the dead. She brought them first to his body, then one of the men led her back out to the living room while the others went about whatever their business was.

"Did your father make any arrangements?" he asked.

"I'm not sure," she answered. "We didn't talk about it."

"Is there anyone else in the family who would know?"

"He didn't tell anyone else."

"Do you have some sense of what he would have wanted?"

He'd already gotten what he wanted.

"I don't think it made much of a difference to him," she said. "He wasn't religious; he wouldn't have wanted a service of any kind. I suppose he should be cremated."

"You don't have to make any decisions right now, if he didn't leave instructions. You should talk it over with your family."

As they spoke the other men came out of the bedroom with a collapsible stretcher. On it was what looked like an oversized garment bag, large and black with a long zipper running its whole length. The first man continued talking, as if to distract her from the sight. She wanted to tell him there was no need; Bill Crane wasn't in that bag.

"Try to get some rest," the man said. "We can speak in the morning."

He handed her his card and followed the group out into the hallway, where they were preparing to navigate their load down the stairs. Sophie shut the door behind them. Once again she was alone.

She hadn't had to worry about any details when it came to her own parents, even though their deaths were so unexpected. Her father had left in his desk a set of papers making clear everything that would be needed, and he'd arranged it all in such a way that she wouldn't have to do the work herself. It was like a script for her to follow, so that in those first days her only job was to hit her marks and know her lines.

Only much later did she think of the strangeness of this. To others it spoke simply of her father's diligence, his thoughtfulness. But few people knew what a troubled man he'd been. It would have been easy enough to accomplish: turning the wheel just a quarter inch. In the worst of her dreams, she saw her mother screaming at him to stop, to guide them back to the road, telling him not to take her with him. Once it had been imagined, the picture never went away. In its wake, all his preparations for their death, the way that everything was already handled for her, took on a frightening significance. Even the buying of the new car, leaving her with the Jaguar, meant something terrible. *Why did the knees prevent me? or why the breasts that I should suck?*

At the grave site her parents were buried side by side, and Sophie was shocked to see how much dirt had been brought from the ground to accommodate them. They had not been large people in life, they had been delicate, and she thought: *It won't take all that much to hold them in the ground; I don't want them so far away.* As the years went by she found herself less and less able to summon the details necessary to keep them present in her life, and she blamed all that dirt. They had been buried too deep.

After the funeral, off the script and asked again to improvise her own life, Sophie no longer felt real to herself. She didn't know what role she ought to play. Even then, her father hadn't left her alone; there was the lawyer, an old family friend named Harvey Green, who had taken charge of everything. He managed the estate still, looked after the Old Manse, which had sat empty all these years.

She wanted very badly to be back there now, to be home. She knew each corner of that odd place as she knew nowhere else in the world. The place knew her as no living thing did. The summer would be over soon; in windswept autumn the Manse was its most beautiful and spirit-haunted. She thought of Rilke's autumn poem: *Whoever has no house now will establish none, whoever lives alone now will live on long alone.*

But there were still arrangements to be made.

Tom had called a few times since leaving. When she hadn't picked up, he'd left messages that she hadn't returned. He wanted just to talk, as though they were old friends in need of catching up. She didn't understand why he should keep calling if he didn't want to come back. What was there to talk about? Then it came to her that he might be trying to determine how much she had discovered in her days with Crane, what she now knew. But she had no plans to tell him this.

He picked up the phone now within a ring, sounding wary.

"Your father died," she said abruptly. "It happened just a few hours ago."

"Oh."

"The man from the funeral home said I should talk with the family about what arrangements would be made."

"I'm not his family," Tom said.

"Maybe," she answered. "But you're mine."

He was quiet for a moment.

"Were you with him?"

"Yes," she said. "Ever since you left."

"I'm sorry, Sophie."

"You don't have to be sorry. I would have come here anyway."

"I mean that I'm sorry about us."

"Are you coming back?" she asked.

"No," he said. "I don't think I am."

"Then don't tell me you're sorry about it."

She felt no particular urge to make things easy for him. Things weren't easy for her.

"Can you give me the name of the place where they took him?"

"It's all right," she said. "I know you don't want to be involved. I just thought that I needed to tell you."

"No," he said. "I should do it. It's not your job. I should have dealt with it from the beginning."

She didn't know how she felt about Tom taking charge of things. It seemed too soon to be done with Crane when either way she'd never escape the consequences of what she'd done. She'd live with it for the rest of her life. Perhaps all that had been meant to happen between them had come to pass. He had arrived as a ghost and left as a ghost. No amount of worrying over his physical remains could make any difference now.

"I need to ask something from you," she said after giving him the number. She hadn't thought, as she was calling, that she had anything to ask. "I want you to take care of the apartment. Our things. Do whatever you want with them. I'm leaving town for a while."

"Are you going to Connecticut?" he asked.

"I think so."

"When are you leaving?"

"In the next few days, I guess."

"Maybe we can sit down and talk before then."

"I'm not sure that there's anything to talk about."

While on the phone, she had wandered into the kitchen. Now that the call was done, she made herself a drink. She brought it back out into the living room and sat down on the couch, sinking into it with exhaustion. There was one thing left, something that had been on her mind several times in the past few days, though she hadn't been able to bring herself to check on it. She collected all the folders and pulled out the ones she had not already read.

She went through them quickly, not stopping until she found the things she was looking for, which she knew would be in there. In the third folder she checked, she came upon a small, one-paragraph announcement, from the *New York Observer*, of the sale of her collection in a two-book deal that included the rights to an as-yet-unwritten novel. The next clip had appeared months later, when the publicity around the collection started to pick up. Every review, good or bad, every printed interview, was there. There was an advertisement announcing a reading she'd given at a bookstore in Soho. How easily Crane might have fit in among the odd older men who attended such readings. Once he saw that Tom wasn't there—an emergency had kept him at work—he might have walked right up and asked her to sign his copy of the book. She imagined she could find that signed copy on a shelf somewhere in the apartment. She might have been disturbed by all this, but she wasn't. She liked the idea that he had been watching on.

The last clipping in the folder was her own wedding announcement, from her hometown paper in Connecticut. In the accompanying photo, she and Tom stood in front of the Manse. After that clipping, it ended. There were more folders, but she didn't bother looking through them. Since there hadn't been another book, there was no more record of her.

If she didn't leave then, she would be trapped forever there. Nothing kept her another moment, except that she was too tired to move. She looked around while finishing her drink. It was a squalid place, really. Not small by the city's standards, not even dirty since she'd been there. But it had the appearance of having been lived in for years by a man who didn't much care for his own life. The world was filled with such people, and Sophie was at the point of becoming one again.

Charlie's book sat on the table in front of her. If she called him, he would take her in without another thought. He would give up anything else, even after all these years. She didn't know where he was living, or how his life was going, but these things would have been easy enough to find out. It probably wouldn't take all that much for them to fall back into their old life. It was presumptuous to think as much, but she knew she was right. Just as she knew that she didn't want that old life, any more than she wanted the life she had now. She picked up the book and held it in her hands.

She kept coming back to the cover, to the young man and woman walking away from each other in the snow. It was not an especially haunting image; it should not have affected her in this way, but it did. She slipped off the dust jacket and let it fall to the floor. She looked now at the red board beneath, with only Charlie's name and the book's title pressed into it. There was something beautiful and timeless to her about a hardback without its jacket, a book that could be known in no way except by reading it. The first thing she'd done when she'd held her own book had been to take the jacket off and see how it looked.

When she stood from the couch, she carried the book with her. She brought it into the bedroom and packed it with the rest of her things. She would bring it wherever she was headed next. She saw the pills in the bag. She ought to have thrown them out, but she took them as well. Also in the bag were the other books she had brought from her apartment. The idea she'd had in those first days, about coaxing from Bill some kind of life-changing confession, struck her as laughable now. He had always been in charge. He had known all along what he wanted from her, and he had gotten it. And he had never cared what she would be left to when he went. It may even have been an added pleasure, to bring her into the fire with him.

The sheets on the hospital bed from which he'd been taken were yellow with his sweat, and they still held the foul smell of his last days. She expected to be repulsed by this, but the bed called out to her, as if it might give her the final rest that it had given him. She climbed in and pulled the sheets up over herself. Despite the smell and the sticky feeling of the dirty sheets against her skin, she made herself stay. It took great effort to keep her thoughts from the pills in her bag. Joining Bill Crane wherever he was would be as easy as that. *For now should I have lain still and been quiet, I should have slept: then had I been at rest.*

Having decided what would come next, Sophie moved quickly. The slightest step from this new course would keep her forever from her goal. She took the bag into the living room and put all of the folders into it. Then she walked out of the apartment, leaving the door unlocked behind her. Nothing left there was of any value to anyone.

Returning to the world, she had some sense of the picture she created. She hadn't showered or changed in days. She was wearing an old T-shirt and no bra. Her hair, which she'd worn short all her life, was growing out awkwardly. She had probably carried some stench even before climbing into his bed; she certainly did now. Anyone she knew, seeing her in this state, would think that she'd gone mad, finally turned feral as she'd all along promised to do.

On the train uptown, the other passengers moved away from her, and it gave her a kind of satisfaction. She imagined running into Tom. It would have been like him to go to the apartment soon after their talk; when charged with a duty, he took care of it. The prospect of seeing him in their old neighborhood didn't move her one way or another. She felt no embarrassment in her condition; she had reached the proper state of humility. She wished to come across a roach somewhere on the street, so that people could watch her take it up and eat it, like John the Baptist feeding on his locusts. But neither Tom nor any bugs happened across her path on the short walk from the subway to the garage.

"O'Brien," she told the parking attendant. "It's the Jaguar in spot 218."

She rarely took the car out, and the attendant wasn't familiar with her. She expected some hassle, looking as she did. But there was none. The man disappeared down the ramp and in another few minutes drove back up and handed over the keys. Sophie tipped him a few dollars, the last she had on hand.

It had been months since she had last driven, heading to New Jersey for Beth's birthday. She was tempted to go that way, to tell Beth about the decision she'd made. She was curious to know what she'd make of it. But the greatest danger now was losing the trail. She had to keep on. She'd made the trip so many times in her life that it was easy despite her exhaustion, despite the hunger that halfway through brought a spell of dizziness. She drove with the windows open—she could hardly stand her own smell— and the whipping of wind kept her attentive and awake.

Pulling into the driveway, she felt a great sense of relief that the house was still there, as though it might have collapsed in her absence. Harvey saw to things, and there were housekeepers and groundskeepers who kept the place always ready for visitors. She could have gone right in, and it would have welcomed her. And she did think of going inside, if only to shower and change before continuing the next leg of her trip. But she decided to present herself as she was: a mendicant, made filthy by the world. She left her bag in the trunk, with the pill bottles and Charlie's book inside. She was sorry to think that she would never read it now, but there was nothing to be done about that. He would have to find some other audience, some other soul for whom to write.

The walk was five miles, the last of them uphill, and it took her two hours. She stopped occasionally at the side of the road and leaned against a post for rest. At one such stop, a horse that had been grazing wandered over and nosed at her curiously. She had nothing to give the animal, but she offered a friendly pat below its eyes. When she reached the point where the road wound its way up the hill, she thought she might not be able to go on. But she continued. She turned onto the dirt road. Her journey was almost done. She kicked up dust as she walked, and it stuck to her sweaty skin.

It was nearly comical, what had become of her appearance. But it wouldn't matter. She knew this, because she could see what was to come, almost all of it. She was going to present herself to them. They would wash her and change her and give her rest. In the morning she would begin preparations. And when the time came, they would welcome her inside the gates, and she would never leave again. She was going to be forgiven. She would give her life for it.

And a life's work it would have to be: she couldn't know until the very last page if she had been redeemed.

Acknowledgements

I don't know that I can express what it means to have a publisher as committed as Tin House Books has been. Tony Perez is a wise and sensitive editor. Nanci McCloskey's intelligence and enthusiasm are more than I deserve. Meg Storey's response to my work meant more than she can know. Some years ago Helen Schulman introduced me to the Tin House family, into which Rob Spillman and Elissa Schappell welcomed me; I'm grateful to call them all friends. And I thank Win McCormack for making it all possible.

At times Sarah Burnes believed in *WHTSW* more than I did. She is not just a dogged agent but a brilliant reader and a rare human being. Never did a call go unanswered or an e-mail ignored, even amid difficult times. My appreciation for her and Logan Garrison and everyone at the Gernert Company is as unflagging as their effort on my behalf has been. Sarah also gave this book its title, by the way.

I have been blessed with great friends, and I thank all of them. I offer particular thanks to those who read this manuscript or otherwise contributed to its completion: Bret Asbury, Millicent Bennett, Brian DeLeeuw, Jim Fuerst, Macy Halford, Dane Huckelbridge, Alexis Rudisill, Benjamin Taylor, and Moira Weigel. The Twin Keys kept me honest.

Thanks to everyone at *Harper's Magazine*.

Much of this book was conceived while I sat beside Mimi Escott in her final months. She gave me not just her permission but her encouragement to make use of the time we spent together in whatever way my imagination saw fit. This was a gift she hardly owed me, but it pales beside the gift of having known her for twenty-seven years. I think of her every day, as I will for so long as I have thoughts to think. I thank her, Sanny Beha, and all the Escotts, Ganses, and Radloffs.

Finally, and essentially, neither this book nor its author could have survived without the love and support of Jim (mon semblable, mon frere!) and Alyson Beha, Mary Alice and Len Teti, or my parents, Jim and Nancy Beha, to whom this book is proudly dedicated. My six nieces and nephews are an endless wonder to me, and the two who will be added to that count by the time this book sees the light of day are an inspiration. You saved me, and I love you all.